FLAMES OF DEATH

Ben stared in horror at the blazing barn. A wild-pitched scream came from inside, a harsh scream of terror. The horses. The life of the ranch.

He yanked hard at the big barn door and violent heat touched his face as the quick draft of fresh air fed the flames, fanning their growth.

The mare was wild in her terror, screaming and circling her burning cell. She reared and struck at the dim figure approaching her. An unshod hoof caught Ben high on the forehead, knocking him to the smoldering straw.

Only just conscious, head pounding, eyes blurred by smoke and blood, Ben knew his shirt was smoldering, that the mare's hide was burning, was conscious of the searing heat from the fire overhead consuming the loft of hay.

And then high above, with a shrieking cry, the roof peak broke . . .

GREAT WESTERNS
by Dan Parkinson

THE SLANTED COLT   (1413, $2.25)

A tall, mysterious stranger named Kichener gave young Benjamin Franklin Blake a gift. It was a gun, a colt pistol, that had belonged to Ben's father. And when a cold-blooded killer vowed to put Ben six feet under, it was a sure thing that Ben would have to learn to use that gun—or die!

GUNPOWDER GLORY   (1448, $2.50)

Jeremy Burke, breaking a deathbed promise to his pa, killed the lowdown Sutton boy who was the cause of his pa's death. But when the bullets started flying, he found there was more at stake than his own life as innocent people were caught in the crossfire of *Gunpowder Glory*.

BLOOD ARROW   (1549, $2.50)

Randall Kerry returned to his camp to find his companion slaughtered and scalped. With a war cry as wild as the savages', the young scout raced forward with his pistol held high to meet them in battle.

BROTHER WOLF   (1728, $2.95)

Only two men could help Lattimer run down the sheriff's killers—a stranger named Stillwell and an Apache who was as deadly with a Colt as he was with a knife. One of them would see justice done—from the muzzle of a six-gun.

CALAMITY TRAIL   (1663, $2.95)

Charles Henry Clayton fled to the west to make his fortune, get married and settle down to a peaceful life. But the situation demanded that he strap on a six-gun and ride toward a showdown of gunpowder and blood that would send him galloping off to either death or glory on the . . . *Calamity Trail*.

Available wherever paperbacks are sold, or order direct from the Publisher. Send cover price plus 50¢ per copy for mailing and handling to Zebra Books, Dept. 1833, 475 Park Avenue South, New York, N.Y. 10016. DO NOT SEND CASH.

FIRE BASIN

BY WILLIAM A. LUCKY

ZEBRA BOOKS
KENSINGTON PUBLISHING CORP.

ZEBRA BOOKS

are published by

Kensington Publishing Corp.
475 Park Avenue South
New York, NY 10016

First printing: May 1986

Printed in the United States of America

To Johnny Holloman,
A good man when you need him

Chapter One

The gray gelding lifted his head abruptly from the icy water, long mottled ears flickering forward and back to pick up on an unexplained sound. Ben Raynor raised himself slightly in the saddle, searching for whatever had caught the mustang's attention. He eased himself back into the saddle, and the flea-bitten gray blew a snort of disgust as the yearling buck thrashed through the bushes lining the far side of the stream. Ben remained still a moment longer, offering the horse a last chance at the clear stream water. The animal swung his large head from side to side, and the light nudge of his rider's legs put the horse down into the rock bed.

Ben Raynor knew he would be early on his business, but restlessness had forced him to break his cold camp in the canyon an hour ago, just after sunrise. Restlessness and an ever-present hunger. By his reckoning he would hit town too early and without enough cash for a meal. He would have a long wait. It was the being broke, so run out that swamping in a saloon looked good, that had finally brought him to the edge of the small Colorado town in answer to the two letters

7

stuffed in his jumper pocket.

The rider shoved his mud-colored hat back and rubbed thoughtfully at his pale forehead. Early sun touched the dark copper of his hair and set it blazing; then the shapeless hat was settled firmly back on his head, and Ben Raynor lined the gray toward the town. The mustang lurched up the far bank of the stream, wove easily through the tangle of alders, and slipped into a lope out onto the level grass beyond.

Raynor let the small horse run briefly, then brought him back down. Even at a walk he would reach town well before anyone was moving much. The gray gave a half-buck at the snug rein, then reluctantly settled into a shuffling walk. Raynor slapped the damp neck. The wiry mustang was the only thing he'd salvaged from his stint of ranching, and the tough animal was contrary enough to last forever.

A sparse grin touched the tired mouth and disappeared as the rider looked ahead in the hazy light to the vague shadows and shapes that spoke of the town at the end of the vast basin, tucked between two white-peaked mountains.

He remembered nothing of this part of Colorado. He'd been born up ahead thirty-four years back, but he knew little about the area, and had no need to learn. The old man whose letter had brought him back had thrown out his only daughter with her newborn child—had let her give birth on the ranch back up in the hills, but hadn't let her stay. And now that child was coming back, to find out what was behind a few terse words written in a faded hand.

Ben shook his head and shifted uncomfortably in the saddle. There was no need to stoke up fresh anger at the old man. He'd grown up with that anger, and had lived with it for years before he could see beyond it. But the past didn't matter anymore. There were other things to feed his anger. Now he would find out what the old man wanted, what was pushing at him to send for a daughter he had disowned years ago. Poor bastard.

Ben grinned at his use of the word. It was a word that he'd lived with for a long time. This poor old bastard was in for a surprise. It had taken seven months for the letters to find him, and another month for him to decide to act. But first the letters had gone in search of Miss Ellie Raynor. His mother.

Ben jerked the mustang back to a slow walk from an eager jig, jammed his hat down hard on the twisted copper curls, and swore softly at the head-tossing resistance from the gray.

George Elliot Ridgeway was a lawyer, liked to think he'd been born looking like a lawyer. He was neat, groomed, shaped and trimmed, barbered and meticulously clothed—all of it done in his image of a lawyer. Even in the early hours just after sunrise, he was dapper and respectable; hair combed, dressing gown tied snug over a soft stomach. His wife believed he had been born to be a lawyer. George Elliot like that.

He saw a political life in his future. A career growing with the state. He would move on to Congress: "The Senator from Colorado, our esteemed colleague." These words were often in his mind, he liked listening to them over and over in the early hours when he could no longer sleep.

9

Ridgeway reached up to brush away the tail end of Nancy's long yellow braid from his eye. Convenience and custom be damned; he wished she would cut short or bind her hair, not braid it to run free in sleep. Every morning it woke him, rubbing his eyes, invading his ear. He pushed the heavy rope aside and eased his bulk from the high feather bed, searching for his carpet scuffs that would be directly underneath his reaching toes.

The rope frame bed sighed and groaned as his weight shifted, and his wife of six years rolled over, her hand reaching out of habit for his back. George touched her forehead and spoke soft, small sounds that left her in deep slumber. For all his fussing, George Elliot Ridgeway did not want his wife to cut her hair or change in any way. She was his perfect wife. He smiled in the dim light and scuffed quietly out.

With brisk and practiced motions, the lawyer started up the stove and set out the coffee to boil, then he carefully combed and dressed, lacking only his suit coat and high shoes to complete the day's picture. Their weight would be added soon enough. George picked up the filled porcelain cup and placed it gently on its saucer. Carrying them carefully, he pushed open the front door to walk out onto the veranda, where he would sit in his chair and sip the hot fragrant coffee. He enjoyed these early mornings, and resented the cold winter which forced him inside, away from the clean air and the first view of his town.

This morning he could see that Arnold Hiller had almost finished painting the Emporium. Perhaps his example would prod the other merchants in Gladstone into giving the entire town a bright new face. He would especially like to see the Feed and Grain cleaned up. Bert Fletcher seemed to think that dealing with animals allowed him a greater mess. Ridgeway snorted his disgust and put the cup down.

The town was growing, changing with the times. Only last week he had finally gotten Ceily Jackman to sign off on the big ranch she had kept going for twenty years, letting it run down, fall apart. It had been a waste of good graze. But now a new cattleman was moving in, had paid cash to the spinster and sent her on her way. The man had a select herd of blooded cattle he was bringing in, and was eager to get his brand going. It was going to be another good ranch in the area, more civilization coming to the town of Gladstone.

The sound of an early morning rider broke into George's musings. Rarely did someone ride into town at this hour. It had to be someone from beyond the basin. It wasn't yet 7:00 AM, and he could hear Nancy starting breakfast, could see other signs of movement in the houses near his, but a rider at this time was unusual.

It was easy to see that the horse was a scrub. Small, thin, uncurried, and mean-looking, an impression enhanced by a roman nose and long mule-like ears. The rider was no better than his horse: dusty, small, brush jumper and pants stained and bleached of all color. A thin bedroll was tied in back of the high cantle, the saddle was badly patched, and the saddle blanket was tattered and faded to a muddy gray. This was not the type of person he welcomed in Gladstone. George sat up on the edge of his chair and began to

11

worry.

There was a strong and simple grace to the rider as he guided the feisty gray down the main street of the slowly awakening town. George prided himself on his judgment of his fellow man, but this one had him baffled. A drifter from the looks of his outfit, a hardcase riding through town looking for almost anything. Yet the man wore no handgun, and the rifle jammed into a rough-made boot under his left leg was old and battered. Not the fighting siderarm for a roughneck.

The searching eyes found George sitting back on the wide, shaded veranda. The man's left hand shifted the reins lightly against the gray neck and the horse came on at an angle toward the lawyer's front porch. The mustang came to a neat halt, and George had his moment to seek out the rider's face before words were spoken.

Older than he had thought, in his late thirties. A man not much in size, with a strong face thinned by hard years. A blunt face framed with high cheekbones, a square jaw, and a blunt nose broken sometime in the recent past. The eyes were faded blue, the color soft and indistinct in the early sun, set deep under a heavy brow, rimmed with dark lashes. The face was drawn and tired, the eyes sunken deep behind a webbing of harsh lines. George started as the man removed the shapeless hat and nodded in his direction. Copper hair lay in matted curls across the man's head, and a thin line of white traced a crooked pattern just above his right ear. His appearance threatened George and his quiet Colorado town.

Ben Raynor had been doing his own looking,

making his own judgments. The man seated so comfortable on the wide veranda, flowered cup placed carefully near him on the small table—this man had to be a success. The padding of flesh on the long face, the soft, smallish hands, the neatly combed brown hair and darker mustache. This man looked to know everyone in this town. Only the feet, stuffed into worn carpet slippers, gave any indication of human weakness.

Ben spoke quickly, just before the man seated on the porch found his voice.

"Looking for a man name of Ridgeway. A lawyer." His voice came loudly in the quiet morning.

"Know where I can find him?"

George Ridgeway was startled. This rider was looking for him. He hesitated, then spoke forcefully, fear making his voice loud and strident.

"A most interesting coincidence, sir. I happen to be George Ridgeway. But my office doesn't open until eight this morning. My wife is cooking breakfast for me right now."

George hesitated again, debating whether or not to invite the stranger to join him. Then he decided. The man was a client of sorts—not a lucrative one to be sure—but a client was a client.

"Why don't you join us for breakfast? It would be no trouble. I'm certain your horse could use some hay and water. Please, sir, do step down."

George regretted his words as soon as he spoke; panic flooded his face and Ben read the signs. It was easy for him to ignore the invitation. He only nodded at the information given, put his hat back on and spoke again, his voice soft.

"At the office, then. Eight o'clock." A pause, then one more question. "Where is it?"

"The office? Oh." George sighed his relief, and pointed out the gilt sign swinging gently halfway down the still-empty street. He thought to speak again, but the rider nudged the small horse into motion and George was left with the view of his stiff shoulders and back as the gray danced sideways toward the sign.

He watched the horse reach the railing in front of his office and stop. The rider stepped down slowly, uncertain and awkward on the ground. He looped the reins twice around the rail and took the two steps up to the wooden sidewalk, clumsy in his high boots. One chair sat in front of the plate window, half-curtains inside pulled closed against prying eyes.

The rider placed himself carefully down on the splintered seat, and returned George's gaze across the distance of the dust-stirred street. With an acknowledging tip of his hat, he leaned the chair back against the wooden window frame and dropped his head, obviously intending to wait there until George made the trip across the street to him.

Ben Raynor's eyes flicked open. The sun's pale yellow was brighter, the blue stronger. He could hear approaching footsteps, and he dropped the chair down hard on the wooden walkway. The loud snap brought him fully awake. It was the lawyer who was taking the two steps up to reach him on the walk. His polished brown half-boots were lightly covered with dust from the crossing.

Ben stood up slowly and stepped sideways as the well-fleshed lawyer inserted a large key into the brass lock and swung the door back, one arm gesturing for his new client to step inside. The two men entered, the client uncertain, the lawyer studiously casual as he walked around behind his desk. The two very different men faced each other over the glossy piece of heavy furniture, and reevaluated their earlier impressions.

George Ridgeway was pleased with himself; the man across from him was as he remembered—hard traveled, worn down, and out-of-pocket poor. He couldn't imagine being able to do anything for him other than hand out a dollar or two. But he would listen.

Ben Raynor was surprised. The well-padded man was younger than he had guessed, and the impression of insufferable pomposity was softened by deep lines of good humor around the full mouth and a touch of easy laughter at the moist brown eyes. Not as stuffy as he had read him, but still a lawyer, and the one whose signature was on the formal letter that had come to him with the old man's thin summons.

Ben sat down in the hard spool-backed chair and waited, his eyes searching the room, while Ridgeway settled behind the desk and went through the motions of clearing and reshuffling papers. Time stretched out long and silent.

It was Ben's slow reaching into his jumper pocket for the letters that finally broke the silence. George Ridgeway cleared his throat and spoke. "Well, sir. What can I do for you this fine spring morning? You look to have come a far distance, and, therefore, there must be a strong and compelling reason that brought you here. Something of importance that you must discuss with me. Please, feel free to speak up."

The trail-worn man's words were as blunt as his face, and not what George Ridgeway had been expecting.

"You sent two letters looking for Ellie Raynor, some time back. Sent them to a lawyer in Gradyville. They caught up with me some four months back. I'm Ellie Raynor's son." He did not leave breathing room for George, but continued his tale. "Your letter said there were legal considerations to be discussed, and the old man's letter talked about making up for the past. Nothing set in either letter. I came to tell you Ellie Raynor is dead. Some two years now."

The words ended, and George Ridgeway was stunned. The man sitting across the desk couldn't be Mister Raynor's heir. Why, he'd been told that Miss Ellie Raynor had been a lovely and gracious young woman, with soft blond hair and a pleasing manner. A kind and generous daughter to Harlow and Netta Raynor.

Certainly a woman of such description couldn't be mother to this somber, hard-faced man. But, then . . . perhaps. The square jaw and the deep-set eyes could have come from Harlow. The high-colored hair and pale eyes could be from the father. No one in this town had ever known who that father was. And now would never know. The delicious shock swept over him again. Harlow Raynor was in for an unsettling surprise.

Finally the lawyer's voice came back to him:

"Well, now. I assume you have proof that you are

16

her son. This is an important matter, not something to be accepted lightly."

Ben had papers, enough for positive proof of his identity.

"Here. A marriage certificate, and letters from Ellie Raynor to my wife. That lawyer in Gradyville thought they would be enough. He knows me from way back."

The harsh face tightened, the pale blue eyes winced from a memory. There was just a flash of expression that startled George with its intensity, then it disappeared. A square hand held out a packet of letters, a picture resting on top. The man started to speak, then his voice broke, a small sound that brought George forward in his chair.

"That picture. It's of my wife and me. And my mother. On our wedding day. Our marriage certificate and a letter from the lawyer, Wixon, sending the letters on to me. He's the one who knew where I'd gone, kept the letters moving after me."

George knew well what the letters contained, could almost recite them by heart. He himself had written to inform the recipient that Harlow Raynor wanted to be reunited with his daughter and any family of hers, and would appreciate it if she would travel to Gladstone at the earliest convenient time. If necessary, he, George Elliot Ridgeway, as lawyer for Harlow Raynor, would advance funds for travel.

And then there was the letter with Harlow Raynor's wavering script, telling the daughter to return, that he was dying and wanted to settle his life. Nothing more than that, nothing reconciliatory. Just a command to return. Now the grandson sat before him, quiet,

17

distant, waiting in the silence.

"I'm sorry about your mother. Mr. Raynor is still with us, although he walks slower every day, and has shut down his ranch and moved into town. I don't suppose you remember anything about the ranch?"

The question was pointless. Raynor's mouth thinned as he shook his head. George continued, "He says he wants to be in town, closer to the preacher and the burying. There isn't much money involved with the estate, but the ranch is to go to his heirs, and he has expressed an interest in seeing these heirs before he dies. He's especially keen to see his daughter. Oh, dear."

The impact of what he had just said hit George. He could only guess at the old man's temper when he heard. Today was going to be difficult.

Ridgeway picked up the soiled pile of letters and carefully unwrapped the oilskin packet to stare at the picture in his hand. He glanced up once at the silent man as if comparing, then looked back at the picture again, studying it for a long time.

It was of three people dressed for a celebration. The man, standing behind two women, was his client; years younger, smiling. Complete in a suit with boiled collar stiff around his neck, hair slicked down and briefly tamed. George glanced up again at the man sitting across his desk. It was hard to see the remnants of the round and eager face he held in front of him in the tired man who sat before him.

In the picture he was standing behind a young woman, her dark hair pulled back on top of her head, her shy smile one of delight. She was small, slender, and pretty, and uncertain in front of the camera.

The woman seated next to her showed hard years: face lined, pale hair streaked with white. But she sat proud, erect, and the young man directly behind her was most definitely her son. And she was Ellie Raynor. Older by twenty-five years than the picture Mister Raynor had shown him, but Ellie Raynor, Harlow Raynor's child. There could be no doubt.

George Ridgeway watched his client's face carefully as he asked the next question.

"This picture, it is of you and your mother? And who is the young woman? What happened to them?"

He was certain the words would bring something to the man's face. He was correct. The wildness flashed bright and hard for an instant in the pale eyes: the wide mouth grew white with tension. But the man showed no signs of answering the question.

George prodded again, knowing he had to have the answer. "Where are they now?"

This time he got a soft answer. He strained to hear the first words.

"The picture is of me and my wife. Day we got married. We didn't expect my mother to be there. Hadn't seen her in almost ten years. But she came to the wedding. Later she lived with us."

The soft voice broke off, the man settled in the chair and took a deep drawing breath, eased his high shoulders.

"That's my wife. She died two years ago. Over in the Arizona territory. My mother died then."

He stopped then, and put his hand across the table. Ridgeway held on to the picture, watching the face so close to his. But he was unprepared for the depth of anger that appeared in the pale eyes.

"I'll keep the picture. The letters are enough for now." The voice stayed soft, but the words were a command. And the hand was steady in front of the lawyer, fingers curled upward.

Ridgeway gently put the faded picture into the cupped hand. The copper-headed man rewrapped the small and brittle paper in the oilskin and returned it to his breast pocket. The two men sat in silence for a short moment, then George brought himself back to his duties—to his two clients: the one sitting in front of him, and the old man back in the hotel room waiting to die.

Chapter Two

"The ranch is the concern here. It is not a big ranch, but one set in a long valley, with good graze behind it and good water. In fact, the ranch has the best water in the basin. There are two springs back up in the hills, providing year-round water. Mr. Raynor has always let his neighbors use the springs when their sources are dry. He settled that ranch almost thirty-five years ago, fought off all kinds of enemies, but he always let his neighbors use the water."

George's pride in his client got caught up in his words, kept him rambling, paying no attention to the emotions battling within the man sitting across the desk.

Mr. Raynor wants his heirs to take over his ranch, work it and keep it going the way he has. Since you are apparently the only heir, what we must do now is to—"

Ben Raynor broke into the flow of words. He struggled with his anger, voice full of pain.

"Want nothing to do with a ranch, or neighbors. Want no part of this. I'm out and gone."

Ben fought to get out of the chair and away from

21

the desk and the bland-faced lawyer, desperate to be outside. He paid no attention to the lawyer's wide-eyed expression of shock.

Finally George Ridgeway found his voice to plead for the old man. "But you are in this now, whether you want it or not. You've ridden all this distance for some reason, and you must at least stay to see your grandfather. That old man wants to settle his life before he dies. You can't just turn him down without speaking to him. You owe him at least that much."

Ben found his feet, and shook his head at the agitated lawyer, his face blank of the passion that had brought him to stand. His voice also held nothing of earlier panic. "You tell Harlow Raynor that repentence came too late, that his daughter is dead and his grandson wants nothing to do with him. Or his ranch."

Then he placed the mud-colored hat back on his head, his motions jerky and awkward, and moved away from the desk. Ridgeway sat still, bewildered by the man standing above him. Who would give up a ranch and refuse to see his only living relative?

Then George found his balance, rose abruptly and took quick steps to reach the door, put out a restraining hand and spoke, his voice edged with urgency and pleading. "Please, you've got to listen. At least meet with Mr. Raynor, give him a chance to explain. You must need money, a horse, something he can give you. Come and listen to him."

Ben wanted to deny what the lawyer said, but reality was too close. He didn't have that dime for a cup of coffee. He could ride out, look for a job down the line, but there would be many more missed dinners before he got there. But if he stayed, at worst, he would get to speak his piece to the old man and still get a meal or two.

"All right. I'll stay for the price of a meal. Come get me when you have the old man, and I'll see him. To talk, but not to stay."

The words were bitter, but for George it was at least a promise of a meeting, a foot in the door. He dug into his pocket and brought out a handful of coins. He proffered them to the grandson, who looked carefully and picked out a one-dollar piece. A quirky smile came to his mouth, but did not touch the pale eyes.

"Come cheap, don't I? A dollar and a promise."

Not expecting an answer, Ben left the office, stopping short just outside the door to adjust to the glare of the morning sun. By its height he'd been inside more than an hour. The old man would probably be stirring soon, and Ben needed breakfast first. He stepped off the walk and went diagonally across the street to a sign that promised breakfast.

The heavy hand knocking at the hotel-room door finally brought Harlow Raynor up from within the stuffed floral chair in a slow shuffle to answer the summons. Nearing eighty years, the old man took all the time he needed to reach the door, figuring it was owed him from the past years when he'd gone as if there wasn't enough time. Before he reached the door it opened, and George Ridgeway stood in front of him, looking as if the dam had broken and hell was pouring through.

"What got you this morning, boy? You 'fraid your

23

past is catching up, or just discovered you ain't got enough past to bother with? What is it, lawyer?"

Harlow Raynor took some delight in the freedom he had earned with old age, a freedom in which folks let him say what no self-respecting person would put up with from a younger man. They just put it down to his mind slipping. Well, let them think that. He liked saying what he knew was true.

The old man's heavy white head was bent, his shoulders stooped, but age could not hide the once-strong body or work-hardened hands. The thought came to George Ridgeway that this man had been a lot taller when he was younger, taller than the grandson waiting somewhere down the street. Now he had to use a cane sometimes, and moved too slowly. But the two men shared the curly hair and square face, even the same break to the blunted nose.

The old man's voice came sharp and clear, interrupting George's musings: "Damn it there, Ridgeway, what makes you pound on my door till it wobbles and then stand there saying nothing. Speak up, boy; I ain't got the rest of my life to wait for you."

George coughed, "Mr. Raynor, a man came to see me early this morning. He had a letter from you in his pocket, one from me, too, that I had sent to Hannibal Wixon in Gradyville. He also had a picture and a marriage license. He says he is your grandson, Ben Raynor."—the old man's face brightened, then shut down as the lawyer continued—"He says your daughter died two years back. His wife died then, too. Didn't say anything about a family, or what happened. He started to leave when I told him your concerns."

24

George stopped for a moment, concerned about the old man standing in front of him. Harlow Raynor waved him on impatiently.

"I was able to talk him into staying in town for a while. He will meet with you. Right now he is eating breakfast. I wanted a chance to speak with you first, to warn you about him. Mr. Raynor, he is a strange man, most adamant that he would not take the ranch."

Ridgeway's flow of words stopped as he took in the trembling of the old man. Suddenly Mr. Raynor looked very old, and fragile.

"Sir, are you all right? Here, sit down."

The old man pulled his thin arm away from the solicitous lawyer and made his way unaided to the overstuffed chair, motioning absently at the unmade bed.

"You, sonny, you sit there and be still. You say my grandson is here, and that Ellie is dead?"

He expected no answer. A drop of moisture squeezed from his eye and got caught in a wrinkle near his mouth. That was all. He went on, speaking more to himself than the pudgy lawyer.

"Didn't figure she would die afore me. That's wrong. What's this boy like? Must look like a Raynor."

George finally had his chance to speak. "He's kind of short, wiry, tough-looking, with dark red hair that has a blaze of white in it. Doesn't say much. I doubt he is going to be much help with the ranch. He reacted very strangely when I started to tell him about the situation."

"Never mind all the talking; go get the boy, or take

me to him. I be getting short of time and don't want to miss out now. Go on, get him. I'll be right behind you."

Ben Raynor had settled in to eggs, ham steak, biscuits, and cups of thick coffee. To finish, he'd had a piece of yesterday's pie that the counterman apologized for. Now he had to hunt up that lawyer and the old man, speak his piece, and move on. The food gave him renewed energy and the day didn't look all that bleak.

He stood at the edge of the boardwalk and leaned up against a post, surveying the town. Folks were moving around now, taking care of their errands. Stores were open, goods changing hands. A small, busy town nearing noontime. Ben wanted no part of town life: he wanted a riding job that asked nothing of him except his body, and that left him too tired for memories.

Ben heard a voice calling his name; he looked down the dark, shadowed walk and made out the fleshy body of the lawyer coming quickly along the boards. Behind him an indistinct figure hurried to keep up; head bent, stick flailing in a vain effort to produce speed. That had to be the old man. His mother's father.

Ben pushed himself away from the post and straightened up, easing his shoulders. A tightening in his belly was the only evidence of his pain.

Ridgeway slowed down the last few steps, suddenly uncertain as to what part he was to play in this meeting. The old man's horny hand pushed him aside, his roughened voice challenging the hard-faced man right in front of him. George Ridgeway stood aside to watch and listen.

"So. You're the young 'un thinks he can put my offer down the crapper. Not that easy, mister. You got born with this one. Now it's your turn."

Ben stared at the shadowed figure. Bitterness flooded him as he recognized years of hard work in the seamed face and the broad, misshapen hands, saw a lifetime with horses revealed in his skinny flanks and bowed legs. A tough old man with a temper to match. He hated this man, had years of hatred built up inside him. But the old man was his grandfather, and he was frail and shaky on bent legs. Ben's anger was too strong to release on this ancient. The old man had no such constraints on him.

"You sure in hell don't look much like your mother, boy, but by damn it you do look like my pap. Nasty old bastard who didn't stay around us kids. Said we all talked too much."

Harlow Raynor watched the copper head raise up, the mouth tighten at the word. So he'd grown up mighty sensitive to that word. Most likely had fought a bunch of kids to hold his pride. The word still hurt, but his boy stood there, quiet like. Seemed to be one of few words.

Then his "boy" broke the hard silence, voice low, temper in check: "Old man, you still talk too much. You've had all the look see and say-so you deserve. Now I'll see you in hell." Ben stood blindly, his ears buzzing, a great feeling of distance and weight coming over him. The ride hadn't been worth the day. He couldn't fight an old man. Didn't much want to fight,

27

just to ride on. He swung sideways and came face to face with the soft lawyer, who reached out a white hand to stop him. The hold on his temper gave and Ben Raynor drove a hard fist into the loose belly of the intruder. Anger running hot, he turned back to the old man who was his grandfather and shook the still-fisted hand in the wrinkled face.

"That belonged to you, old man. That and more. For all the hell you birthed. But it's too late for me, and for you."

He glanced briefly at the fallen lawyer. Ridgeway had hit the splintery boardwalk hard on his backside, arms wrapped protectively about his assaulted stomach. His coat had flown back, and several coins had rolled from the shallow side pockets of his pants to spill across the slatted walk. Ben heard the jingle, and reached down to pick up the rolling money. He lifted a wintery face to the silent old man, and held out a handful of coin.

"My fee for staying to talk to you. Tell Ridgeway thanks."

His pale eyes held no connection to the grin on his mouth; instead they contained fire with no warmth, a promise of banked violence. He shoved the coins in his pocket and stepped by the fallen man. A tilted sign further down the walk told of the "Texas Star," offering a bottle and solitude.

Chapter Three

There were enough people on the street who witnessed the confrontation that word went through the small town like a cold wind from the peak. At his Emporium, Arnold Hiller was the first to guess aloud that the man who had just been confronted by Harlow Raynor and George Ridgeway had to be Ellie Raynor's son, old Harlow's grandson. The old man had not been shy about his search, and everyone in the small town knew. And anyone who did some thinking had realized that the meeting would not be sweet and social. Now George Ridgeway would testify to that.

But Arnold Hiller tried to be a good man, not a gossip, not one to speculate for long on such things that were out of his jurisdiction. Later that day he would take his thoughts home to his wife and they would go over the possibilities. So he turned his beefy hands to the task of cutting out the six yards of blue cloth that Emily Chapman was waiting for. His bald head glistened in the growing warmth of the spring day. By nightfall he would be covered with bits of colored lint, dust, and perhaps ink and a few stray flecks of candy. He sold everything in his store.

The two women at the counter had seen the set-to on the boardwalk, and preferred to ignore it. Emily Chapman and her sister, Nora Stuart, barely listened to Mr. Hiller's comments. They knew the old man; they lived up in the foothills near his empty R Cross ranch. He had been their neighbor, kind and friendly the few times they had visited, but mostly they kept to their own ranch. And they did not want to hear the speculation about the strange red-headed man and his fight out on the walk.

Emily Chapman had come with her sister when she married Walter Stuart seven years ago, and the three of them had worked the small ranch long and hard to keep it alive. When the push was eased, when they had actually had enough cattle to sell and pay off the debts, Walt had died. Had gagged slightly just after lunch one day, leaned back in his chair, and died.

That had been three years ago. Now Emily and Nora did the ranch work, kept track of the cattle, raised the foals from Walt's prize band of mares. They had chosen to stay at the ranch, to work for their small piece of land—Nora because it had been Walt's choice, his dream; Emily because there was no place else for her.

Voices out on the street came to Emily, brought her back from daydreaming. She turned back to business and put the ugly incident from her thoughts.

Inside the saloon, solitude was offered for the price of a bottle. Ben Raynor was the only customer; it was early yet in this law-abiding town and the men were working. The bartender immediately brought out a

30

glass and poured one drink from a full bottle. Before he could put the bottle back under the counter, Ben stayed his hand and threw down three of Ridgeway's one-dollar pieces.

"I'll drink up this much, then you tell me how drunk I am and we'll go from there."

Not quite understanding the words but recognizing the value of the coin in front of him, Herb Austin nodded his agreement and backed away. He'd figured out early in his career behind the bar to leave the quiet ones alone, to take their money, and call the law only if they caused trouble. He ran his eyes over the slight man leaning on the bar, staring at the amber-filled glass raised just above the shiny wood.

It was Herb's educated guess that this one would drink alone, ignore the surroundings, and then leave quietly, unnoticed by the swelling noontime crowd. Herb sighed his relief—until the copper-haired man raised his eyes to meet Herb's, pale eyes that dug into Herb, eyes that held a ghost. Herb turned his head and wiped at a spotted glass. He was afraid. This one would fight for certain. Today. He sighed and looked over his shoulder at the brand-new mirror covering the wall.

The bite of the alcohol broke the first layers of anger in Ben, softened the tight belly, eased the shallow breathing. Another drink poured and swallowed, and he could feel the painfully tight muscles across his back loosen their hold. He stared at the bartender; the man looked away, then rushed to serve another customer. The third drink put all misplaced thoughts about home and family from his mind. . . .

Ben looked in wide-eyed astonishment when the

31

barkeep came back to remove the almost-empty bottle, tilting his head in obvious question. Son of a gun wanted more money. Fair justice to have the most respectable George Ridgeway pay for a midday drunk. He searched with thickened fingers through one pocket and then another before he found the last two coins. He slammed them down on the bar.

"Same agreement: you let me drink till these are done, then we'll settle."

No point in telling the barkeep that all his money now lay between them on the highly polished wood.

The noise next to him was a surprise. Ben turned slightly to check the source and, off balance, he pushed against an arm. The arm shoved him back hard, jamming his ribs into the rounded bar edge. Ben coughed against the shock and turned slowly. A need rode him now, a need to strike out against the morning's pain. Herb Austin saw his face, looked at his neighbor at the bar, and frowned. The pale-eyed man had found his fight.

The tall man looked down to Ben, saw a half-raised hand holding a full shot of liquor, saw the anger hot in the square face and, grinning, took up the challenge. He drove his elbow into Ben's forearm, spilling the last of Ridgeway's whiskey contribution over Ben, soaking his shirt-front and stinging his eyes. The tall man smiled; that insult would guarantee him a fight, and the nature of his opponent—slight, drift poor, and drunk—guaranteed him a victory. Mont Hackett grinned his pleasure and turned to his refilled beer glass raising it in a mocking salute to his drinking companion, Lug Bremen. He turned away from Ben.

Reflex drove Ben's loosely bunched fist to the side

of Hackett's neck. The instant pain brought Hackett around angrily to face his attacker. He had thought to take the first blow. Lug Bremen turned his focus away from the beer glass in front of him when he heard the familiar war whoop. Somehow a fight had started, Hackett was in the middle, and he had missed the beginning.

The two men were long-time partners in brawling. Bremen winked at Hackett after assessing their opponent. This one didn't offer much entertainment for the two of them. Just enough to work up a sweat for another beer. Bremen chose to pick up his beer and drain it before entering the fight. He had not read the unleased fury in his partner's opponent, the temper worn thin by a long hungry ride and then a quick end to reborn dreams.

Mont Hackett stepped back, off balance from a hard fist driven deep into his belly. In quick succession Raynor struck the larger man with punching blows to his unprotected mouth and gut. Just outside his vision, Ben saw a glint of metal as Lug Bremen came alive. The bright metal of a gun barrel caught Ben's eye just before it reached the side of his head. He twisted violently away, but not far enough, and the barrel dug hard into the junction of his shoulder and arm, sending him to his knees, numbing him with the pain. The blow would have crushed his skull. Ben fought to rise, struggling to gather his body to move.

A red face came close to his, an ugly round face belonging to a squat, evil-smelling man—a face leaning down to check the damage. Then the face disappeared and a heavy boot slammed into Ben's side, sending him sideways, still at the mercy of the first stunning blow. Ben rolled with force, knowing that the next kick would tear him apart. He went down and over and away from the booted foot and came up fast, dazed but able to fight.

The three antagonists broke apart. Ben stood loose and hunched, swaying gently. Lug Bremen glanced anxiously at his partner, saw his sign, and moved quickly to the left. But before he was set a wild man came at him, knocking his hat free, bloodying his nose.

Hackett moved in fast to pull the smaller man off Bremen, and Ben came around hard, his fist going unerringly into Hackett's hanging paunch. A pick-up blow from Bremen caught Ben on his bruised shoulder, setting up a howling protest from damaged nerves. His right hand lost feeling, but Ben did not lose his momentum.

He rammed his body into Bremen, driving the red-faced man back into the crowd now surrounding the fighters. Bremen rolled underneath Ben, wrapped himself around the bucking form, and hugged with rock-hard arms. Hackett caught up to the rolling bodies and waited for his chance.

Trapped on top of the squat puncher, arms tight at his sides, Ben fought to get free, then butted the top of his head repeatedly into Lug's already tender nose. The man yelped with pain, then a heavy blow took Ben in the ribs. Lug's tight hold kept him in place; another kick cracked ribs, a third brought instant bright agony to Ben's lower back. Darkness tunneled in on his vision, leaving only a narrow line. At the end he could see a crimson nose.

Another kick, again into his weakened ribs, drove

the darkness away, loosening a bright spark of demonic fury deep in the trapped man. These kicks would kill him. Ben turned his head and found Lug's ear with his teeth. They sank deep into the fleshy lobe, and he was rewarded with another howl of pain and a loosening of the wrapped bands holding him prisoner. He rolled across the thick body beneath him, close to freedom.

The next kick skimmed across his back and drove the weakened arms away. Ben rolled with the force of the kick, spun up onto his feet and dove blindly at the unprotected belly of Mont Hackett. His head sank deep into bulging flesh, and he was rewarded with a shower of blood and foul breath as he rammed Hackett up against the bar.

A shot shattered the awed silence, then another. A strong voice reached through the fury in Ben. His opponents, grudgingly respectful of the power behind the voice, tried to back off from the bloodied man who fought them. Ben had no such restraint, felt none of the power. He pushed past a bulky shape and drove his fist into Bremen's face, sending the man sprawling back into the subdued crowd.

A heavy hand grasped Ben's shoulder; a hard voice told him to turn around. He twisted to get free of the pressure, but gave in as he finally felt the weight.

"That's enough of that, mister. You stop the fight. These two have had more than enough. Looks to me like you busted them in two. Enough."

The voice wasn't threatening, or even annoyed. Just tired. Ben stepped back and eyed the law. He saw a barrel-chested man headed into middle age, with thinning brown hair and a heavy nose. The man looked solid, dependable. Just right for this town.

Cable Orton shook his head. He knew how Hackett and Bremen met their fights. And they usually won. But this man before him had come head-on to their kicks and had torn the two apart. Orton knew that the man had absorbed a lot of punishment, could read the blood-streaked face and hunched back, but this time the matched pair had received their share, and more. Hackett's face was covered with blood and mucus from his nose, and Bremen's hand stayed protectively over his torn and dripping ear. Both men were subdued by their battle.

Orton wanted a good look at the brawler who had taken these two.

What he saw in the bruised face of the slight man made him hesitate, and re-evaluate his quick judgment. He had lived his years depending on that judgment being correct. This wasn't just a drunken cowpoke swaying before him. There was no bravado to the small man, only a clear go-to-hell look that delivered trouble.

He'd seen a few men with that look; indifferent to what was around them, uncaring. Eyes with nothing behind them. Some of these men were killers, some were men who had lived with too much. Orton didn't know where this one fitted, and if he handled things right he would never need to know.

It was the eyes that gave him away, the marshal thought. Bremen and Hackett had never had a chance. The marshal spoke, his careful voice clearing the air.

"I talked to Herb; he says it was Hackett who spilled some booze, that this one here took the offensive and then Bremen got into the act. Anyone got anything different to say?"

He waited while the soft murmur of the crowd grew and then settled, with no one finding much to say. Satisfied, Orton turned to the bloody man who had made no move to defend himself. He felt some shame at his words, but there was no other choice. This town didn't need a man like this one. It was a peaceable town, and would stay that way.

"You. Get out. Ride on now and there will be no charges."

Cable Orton made a bet with himself as he spoke the uncaring words, and he won. There was no reaction in the pale eyes, neither relief nor anger, just cold acceptance of the order. He was right about this one. Didn't give a damn about anything. He would be glad to see the man ride on.

Ben moved very slowly, cautious of the fire in his ribs. Each breath jabbed at him with a pointed end. It would be a wonder if he could get on the gray. He walked outside into the bright sun, and stopped in a haze of pain as he bumped into an unseen post. His audible grunt reached the two women walking down the short steps to their team and wagon.

Two heads turned in instant sympathy, but the brief flare of pity died as they saw the saloon doors shaded behind him, the obvious signs of a fight. Drinking and brawling when a man should be working. The two sisters moved on, the plain one picking up the lines from the railing and climbing into the carriage with her sister. One word from her and the team stepped out into the activity of the main street.

Ben found pleasure in watching the woman handling the lines. She knew her horses. Then he was alone with the pain. He knew he had to face the ugly-tempered gray gelding. He reached the mottled shoulder and stood there, flatfooted and hunched against his ribs. The horse sensed weakness in his rider and leaned hard against him, stamping his platter feet, thrashing the ratty tail.

The cracked ribs were bearable until Ben raised his arm to touch the horn; then he dropped his hand to lean his forehead against the cool leather of the saddle. The gray quieted for that moment, then shoved rudely into Ben's middle, bringing all the hurt alive again.

He could hear voices coming near him, calling his name. He resented that intrusion, knowing that he wanted no one in this town to call him. He resisted the oncoming pain and swung quickly into the saddle. The gray gave him no chance to catch his breath, but swung around over his hocks and struck a high lope out into the street. All that was left to Ben was to hang onto the horn with both hands and ride through the misted pain.

Chapter Four

The tight-springed farm wagon skipped over a deepening rut, and Emily Chapman slid sideways on the board seat, jamming her sister hard in the side. The loosely wrapped parcel in her hand bounced off the near mare's rump and rolled to the side of the road. Nora's right hand came up and back with the impact, jerking the off mare in her mouth. The team jumped forward at the unexpected dual attack, and took the opportunity to stampede into a blind run.

Emily righted herself through the brief panic as she felt the team take hold, and then watched her sister wrestle with the chunky mares. Nora would handle this. Fifty feet down the road, the team came to a ragged halt, heads see-sawed out of rhythm to stop their run.

The two women sat with shoulders just touching on the narrow seat. Nora was the older and steadier of the two. Just twenty-one when she met and then married Walt Stuart, she was facing her thirty-first birthday as a widow. Fine, straight, dark hair, tucked back and pinned up, had struggled loose in the abortive runaway. Speaking softly to the mares, Nora released one rein to ineffectively push the hair back in place. Briefly and rebelliously she considered how practical short hair would be.

Nora smiled at Emily, noting the fine line of perspiration on her upper lip, the blanched color to her cheeks. The easing of tension in Nora's dark eyes, the relaxing of the tight lines in her worn face, gave the plain etched features a quick touch of beauty. Nora's eyes were brown and gently lashed, her nose too strong, her jaw well defined and muscled, her mouth bracketed with lines. Her eyes held the key: quick to turn harsh and judgmental, slow to soften in smile.

Emily Chapman was two years younger than her sister, and wildly beautiful: dark hair rich and thick, brow smooth over blue-violet eyes lined with impossibly long lashes. Her face was smooth and balanced, with heightened cheekbones and a firm, lush mouth. Where Nora's body was hard muscled and angular, Emily was rounded, inviting, a womanly shape that could not be covered by the well-worn men's shirts and shapeless pants she wore.

Emily fought her beauty and the easy attention it brought her. Nora took no notice of men and kept to her work. She had loved Walt well, and his death was beyond her understanding. Emily was loved by all men, and knew no trust in their feelings and words. Or in her own.

She stepped down from the wagon to retrieve the fallen package. It contained the material for Nora's birthday present, a rich vivid cut of blue cloth to make her a new dress—a pretty dress to remind Nora that she was still a young woman. Emily smiled to herself as she picked up the dusty package; tomorrow evening Nora had promised they would go to the dance at the schoolhouse. And Emily would have this new dress ready for her.

Settled back on the seat, Emily watched Nora's strong hands guide the still-jumpy mares back onto the road and urge them to a good trot homeward. They were both a little anxious to know if the new hand was going to work out, and they would know as soon as they came into the yard. He had been left with specific instructions on repairs to the corral gate, had been told to have it done before they returned. This would be the deciding test. And Emily felt he would fail.

Finding and then keeping a good hand was difficult for the two women. With little spare cash, they could offer only low wages and good cooking. The majority of the riders drifting through assumed they could take more. They would meet with Nora, agree to the work and the wages, then find Emily—and the trouble would start.

Emily had once suggested leaving, finding work in a town. But both sisters knew what "other work" would lead to. As a schoolteacher, or in a store, wives would begin to talk as their husbands and sons spent more and more time with the new woman. Visits, gossip, one incident and Emily would be on the move again. The best solution—the only solution—was for her to remain on the secluded ranch on the edge of the wide basin and struggle along with whatever hired man they could find, or none at all.

Blake Morse had worked hard on that section of corral. He stood back to admire the results. The

41

gatepost still leaned some, maybe too much, but the gate stayed latched now, and it would take a fair push from a big horse to break it away again. He jimmied the last hinge back into place, using a scrap of shaved wood pushed deep into the hole to tighten its grip. It would take too long to fix the hinge properly, and wouldn't leave him enough time to get cleaned up before the two women returned.

He ran a hand reflectively through blond wavy hair. This spread wasn't a bad place. With a strong man to run things, it would be a real moneymaker. There was a good herd of cattle grazing out in the small valley, and that bay stud up in the back hills produced some fine horseflesh. Old Mister Stuart must have had a good eye.

All he needed was to get that older sister off by herself, spend some sweet words coaxing her, and the ranch would be his. Morse's loose mouth widened to a leer as he envisioned his plans. It was the younger one who drew his attention. That lush body trying to hide under too-big shirt and pants didn't fool him; he could see the heavy breasts, the narrow waist and rounded butt. That was his woman, but first he had to tend to the widow. She was already broken in, would be easy to retrain. Then he could have them both.

Blake Morse was a big man, and by his reckoning a handsome one. Enough of the ladies had told him so. Blond hair, the kind women liked to play with, heavy brooding eyes, smooth features marred only by a slackness to his mouth. He knew how to talk to the ladies, had picked up the rudiments of manners, enough to be passable in company. He'd look might good riding that big bay stud house, and would be able to do that soon. After he rode the fillies.

Nora drew the team of mares up by the gate. A quick sigh escaped her lips. She didn't need to say anything to Emily, just shook her head slightly as she wrapped the reins around the whipstock. Emily caught the set to her sister's mouth and jumped from the wagon seat. She headed straight to the house, her long strides showing a sense of urgency. They had the next few minutes already planned and rehearsed. It was a too-familiar pattern.

The grey's temper did not improve. It was as if the horse resented the flopping burden in the saddle and was working all the angles short of actual pitching to rid himself of his rider. Side and back on fire, head pounding, the dried blood itching his face, Ben Raynor managed the half-rears and jolting lurches of the mustang.

In a very detached portion of his mind, Ben found humor in the gray's antics. The wiry mustang had no pity for anything weak. And so the silent battle went on: the small ticked horse fought for his head, shied from nothing, half-reared. Time and again the rider pulled tight on the short-shanked curb bit, laid spurs to the shaggy sides, hauled the big head around by the rawhide bosal. He could look hard into the white-rimmed eye of his opponent. And he could have sworn that the bastard horse winked at him.

In this manner the horse and rider progressed slowly and tortuously down the rutted path away from the town of Gladstone.

A strong yank brought the head around again. This

time the jerk caught a half-rear and unbalanced the gray, staggered him, and brought horse and rider down flat on the dust-covered road. With his head pulled tight against his shoulder, the gray could not get up. Raynor's right leg was under the small body, lying inside a deep rut. There was little pressure from the gray's body on his leg, and lying quiet for a moment eased the torment of his ribs. Ben drifted in his thoughts, enjoying the respite from the continuous battle.

But the gray hadn't quit. The animal drew up his left hind leg and kicked wildly at the booted foot of the rider laying alongside his belly. The abrupt motion caught Ben unprepared; his hand slipped on the wild-eyed head still jammed up against the sweaty shoulder, and the gray lurched up to his freedom in a short scramble that shook Ben from the saddle. His right foot had been scraped free of the stirrup in the fall, and his left boot was dislodged in the gray's last kick.

When the mustang reached his feet, he was without the burden of a rider. A high squeal accompanied a deadly backwards kick, and the small gray horse bolted down the road.

It would be easy to stay in the rut, cradled by the dust-softened ground. Ben lay there for a heartbeat longer, struggling to ease his breathing. Finally, reluctantly, he started the fight to get up, and once on his feet he stared down the road at the slowly settling dust where his horse had disappeared. A deep sigh left him, ending in a stab of pain from the cracked ribs.

Ben jammed the battered hat back on his aching head. There was nothing left to do but walk. Occa-

44

sionally he could make out the hoofprints of the mustang; they were spread wide apart, in long fast strides, running free. The gelding had kept to the side of the road at a furious gallop, every so often letting out a wild buck in celebration.

After a mile, the tracks veered sharply from the road. The runt was headed toward a high vee formed by the surrounding mountains. Ben bet he would never see the horse, or his gear, again. Absently he patted the small bulge in his chest pocket, checking the safety of the oilskin wrap.

The track he followed wound through the center of a wide valley, parklike with its high wide-topped pines and undergrowth of good grasses. The land was enough to give heart to any drifting cowhand harboring ideas of his own ranch. The valley rose and dropped in swells, tantalizing a traveler with promises of more just beyond the next rise. Ben did not see the rich land he walked.

Another staggered mile and Ben Raynor knew for certain that his brief stint as a foot soldier was doomed. His broken boots offered no support, and the unaccustomed march had swollen his feet to thickened stumps inside the tight leather.

A shallow pair of ruts diverged from the main road; fresh tracks and lightly settling dust suggested recent passage. Knowing someone or something was ahead was better than walking to the unknown, and was much preferred to the tired-faced lawman who read him so easily and the cranky old man back in the town.

The path wound sharply around a close set of pine, then the low outline of ranch buildings could be seen lying in a large natural yard among the alders and pine fighting the prairie grasses. Walking closer, Ben could see figures moving across the yard.

Finally he could make out a big man being prodded none too politely by a very angry woman. Another woman stood beside a slanted corral gate. A change in the shadows, and he could see the faces clearly: fury sharp in the one woman's face, high red covering the man's handsome features as he hurried to place gear on a rangy sorrel bronc. Ben rested against the far corral fence and listened.

"Out, Morse. You've been a fool for your thoughts. We don't let one such as you near us. Ride on and don't look back." The woman's words were backed by a deft cradling of a well-oiled shotgun.

But Blake Morse wasn't going to be ordered about by a woman. He reined the sorrel around to face the two women, his intentions clear across his livid face. Before he could drive spurs into the gelding's sides, a blast of buckshot beside his head stopped him. With the killing echo burning in his ears, Morse swung the long-legged horse in a tight circle and drove the animal out of the yard with harsh jabs to its sides. The sorrel obliged with a back-snapping plunge that took horse and rider beyond the still figure beside the corral fence, just brushing thin shoulders as Ben twisted aside.

The silence that followed did not dissipate the fury riding Nora Stuart. She turned to the man who had leaned so casually on the corral fence to watch the proceedings. She wanted no truck with any fool who thought he could walk in here uninvited and take over from Morse. Her first words carried a strong holdover from the recent violence.

"You too, mister. Out. Got no place for more of you bums here. This is a *working* ranch."

Anger underlined the word *working*. She had had enough of slackers. Nora motioned with the lowered shotgun, then stopped. She recognized the man from town—the fighter thrown out of the Texas Star. Disgust filled her eyes, and she raised the barrel slightly, to remind Ben of her words.

He had heard, had accepted his dismissal. But it was taking him time to get moving, to push away from the supporting fence and face that walk ahead. He glanced briefly at the other woman who had come closer, then dipped his head in acknowledgment of the order and took one step toward the road.

"Nora, wait, hear him out. You didn't give him a chance. Please listen."

Ben Raynor stopped and turned to stare at the woman who championed him. Pale eyes met blue-violet ones; he nodded again at the beautiful woman and looked back to Nora. She was the one who would make the decision.

Indifference to her beauty was a rare experience for Emily. Yet this copper-headed man had looked at her and turned away, had stared into her eyes and beyond them, not seeing an invitation in them.

Nora watched the silent exchange, waited as Ben Raynor took that one step toward her, then stood easily while she looked him over. He stood patiently under her scrutiny, carrying neither bluster nor pretense in his wait. Quiet, contained, he held her gaze and offered her nothing.

She was right. It was the fighter from earlier in

town. She marked the bruise on his jaw, the blood crusted on his brow; this was the man gossip said was Mr. Raynor's grandson. Two fights in town in one morning. Common sense said to send him down the road, but curiosity warred to hire him.

Ben spoke to the plain woman. "Plain to see what needs doing with that gate, Ma'am." There was a long pause after the surprising sound of his words. Then, "I can fix that easy. Fix most anything around a ranch."

Ben wanted to say more, to list his skills. He needed this job. But pride and an inner reluctance kept him silent. She would run him off if he begged.

Sharp words came to Nora, but she shut them down. Something in this man pricked her hard. She watched his wide mouth pull tight, saw the pale eyes turn away from her. He was desperate for this work. Almost as desperate as she was about finding a hired man. Her voice came quick on top of his words.

"What's your name? . . . at least something we can call you by."

"Ben, ma'am, Ben Raynor." He thought to lie, but it was his name, and he had been proud of it in the past.

He is the grandson, Nora thought. A rare and charming smile touched her face, lightening the severity of its lines. She always thought of grandsons as twelve years old and in knee pants. This one could be forty, had a hard look to him that didn't go with whittling and fishing holes. She nodded to Ben: the job was his.

The sisters came close to watch their new hired help walk awkwardly to the small shed tacked on the side of the barn. Inside he would find a rope bunk and a few nails for his gear. Nora caught the confusion from her sister and answered her unasked question.

"It's easy, Em. The man doesn't care about us. You saw. He don't seem to care about much at all. But he looks to know what he is about. His hands are hard-calloused; he saw what needed to be done. A good change from Morse and the others. Tell him what time supper will be. I'll put up the mares."

Nora walked to the patient team, the sweat dried on them in a salted crust. Her voice came back to Emily, drawing the woman from her thoughts:

"I'll need a jacket, got to go up and bring down those late mares. Don't want them foaling out in chancy weather. You keep your eye on this one; I'll be back before dark."

The whole damned gate had to be taken down and rehung. The effort needed to line up the gate against the post to sight for the new hinge placement wrenched a shocked grunt of pain from Ben. The gate slipped from the blocks of wood he'd set up to balance it, and thudded on the corral floor, sending the three geldings inside off in a panicked run. Bent double against the bite from his ribs, Ben leaned against the crooked post and watched the confusion.

A light hand on his shoulder brought Ben upright in a spin, and a barely audible sigh echoed the grimace across his face. Emily Chapman watched the tightening as the man fought for control, and admired the effort that wiped clean the pain.

"You need help with this."

49

It was a simple statement, with no hint of uncertainty. "I can balance the end while you set the gate and mark the hinges."

Ben nodded and stretched carefully to get a hand under the heavy, wooden-framed gate. Emily tugged at the other end of the unwieldy object, and together they rested it on the blocks, aligned it to the reset post. With the gate held firm by her strong hands, Ben marked and set the new holes. Then together they lifted the gate just enough to let it swing easily, and he finished setting in the hinge.

There was no denying her beauty. Even hard at work, the dark blue-violet eyes glowed, and the dust and sweat mingled on her face did not mar the perfect skin and ripe mouth. Nothing could hide her body. The slightest move accentuated her breasts, tightened the fabric across her hips, highlighted the smallness of her waist.

Ben Raynor watched the woman, worked next to her, smelled her sweetness, and found no response in himself. His wife had been beautiful. And his wife was dead. There was nothing more for him.

Nora let the blue dun take the bit and run. It satisfied her, eased the tension from the trip to town and the scene with Morse. Reluctantly she reined in the blue and circled five heavy-bellied broodmares who looked up placidly at her approach. From far down the high, secluded valley, a solid bay stallion tipped his ears forward and whistled a questioning challenge.

Nora yelled "*Yaah* Duke" at the slowly trotting

bay, and the stallion circled and returned to the mares and foals in his protection. He recognized her authority. She flipped her coiled rope at the mares, and one dark-red lady lifted her head as if in answer. Then the mares lined up slowly, and walked ponderously along the well-defined path that would take them down to the home ranch.

Nora smiled as she watched the mares walk into the ranch yard. Emily and the new man had been busy. The gate was rehung, the post reset, and the geldings had been moved out to give the mares their pen. She smiled again as she watched the overdue mothers settle in to mounds of hay waiting for them. This was hers and Emily's future.

She rode the blue to the barn, stripped the horse of his gear and hung it without thinking, then turned the blue out with the other geldings. Supper lay ahead, then a night with the books, and a new day. Spring cheered her, drove aside for a while the fear of losing the ranch, of being unable to beat the deadline at the bank. She absently wiped her arm across her forehead, leaving a streak of sweaty grime.

Emily was waiting at the back door as Ben came to stand outside. The smell of beef stew and hot biscuits had brought him in from the barn. Nora sat at the table and ignored the waiting shadow outside the door. She too was hungry.

"Come in, Ben. Don't mind Nora. She's still mad at that stupid Morse. Pay her no mind."

Nora looked up in annoyance at her sister's prattling. There was no need to explain her actions or moods to the hired help. But she did smile at Ben slightly, allowing that he did have the right to come inside and eat. Part of the meager pay was good meals.

Being inside the warm kitchen near the two women busy with their chores brought back thoughts Ben wanted kept buried; he'd spent a long time digging them under. Only hunger kept him inside the small room. He sat on the edge of a wobbly chair and ate, his head down, concentrating on the task and ignoring all attempt at talk.

Nora felt her temper rise. *Damn* this man for refusing to answer simple questions. She didn't want much, but she owned the right to some answers about him. He was eating her food and living on her ranch; she needed something to ease her fears.

"I said, are you related to Harlow Raynor? The old man in town? He was our neighbor up here till he moved in. A good neighbor. We never saw him much, but we knew he was there."

Ben looked up at the words. His pale eyes went from sister to sister, taking note of the startling, subtle differences between the two. He was unwilling to speak, but the faces nagged him, dug a concern out of his conscience. The needed some reassurance from him. His voice was soft and slow:

"Grandson. Wanted to give me the ranch. Don't want it. Guess he'll sell now. I'm leaving soon as I work off a horse and gear." He remembered his manners and added, "Thanks. Good meal."

Ben pushed back the chair and stood. Hat in hand he went outside to the clear air and deepening shadows of nighttime. A short walk across the yard to the small, cheerless room, and he sat on the sagging rope bed, letting the sounds of the barn animals, their sharp comforting smells, wash over him and take away the day. He spent slow and painful time removing boots from swollen feet, grunting with the effort needed to bend over. Then he was stretched out on the lumpy cot and asleep in minutes.

Chapter Five

"That there son of a bitch is pure ugly."

Windy Dawes, long-faced, long-bodied, thinning grey hair covering a high-domed forehead, as ugly as the critter he faced, was the only man who dared to speak such thoughts in the presence of the ugly son of a bitch's owner, Perce Tolliver. The ruddy-faced cattleman gave a snort at his old compadre's comment. That there "son of a bitch" was a purebred, red-headed, curly-coated durham bull, expensive by any pocketbook, and ugly only to those eyes that still held appreciation for the old longhorn.

Perce Tolliver was teaching his eyes to read the grace of the stubby-legged critter before him. He was finding the education easy. Translate the bulk before him into more meat and higher profit on the hoof, and the small-eyed bull became beautiful. It amazed him how something so ugly could become so perfect. Sort of like a homely woman with a new, and large, fortune.

The two men sat their horses while a dusty ranchhand slammed shut the reinforced gate that held the lowering bull. Shorthorns weren't noted for their good temper, in that they were blood kin to the longhorn. Perce slapped the bowed neck of the high-blooded black he sat. The horse shined so much his coat reflected the silver conchas hammered into the breast collar snugged up against his chest. Perce Toliver put his money back into his stock, and spent damned little of it on himself.

His face showed the years and the hard times behind him. In his mid-fifties, face seamed and lined from the miles he'd ridden and the fortunes he'd lost, Perce Tolliver was a hard man, a driver of those around him. He'd started small some thirty years ago, had worked up to a fine ranch stocked with hundreds of tough longhorns, only to watch them die in back-to-back winter freeze-ups. He had moved then from the Montana cold to the Arizona territory, and had rebuilt his spread—only to lose again to the heat which had mercilessly baked his herds and burned his range.

But that was the past. It had taken a long time to rebuild the second time, to reeducate himself in the new techniques, to find better range that suited him. Never again would he be totally at the mercy of weather. This southern end of the great mountain range offered good streams, strong spring runoff, mild winters, and a reasonably dry summer. This time there were fewer cattle, but they were cattle bred for more meat. He protected them with late-cut winter hay and irrigated fields. And there were springs, constant springs, to take them through the summer heat.

The springs. Water was the key. Constant water that only he controlled. He had worked this range years ago, been fired from here, knew of the springs tucked behind the razor-sharp hills. And knew that the ranches controlling these springs were vulnerable. The old man was finally dying, his ranch waiting for a forced sale. Perce had already bought out the Jackman place. Its headquarters were in the high country, near the springs, and would be *his* headquarters for now—until he controlled the springs. The Stuart ranch was left, the ranch run by two women.

Perce snorted, disgust deep in his light gray eyes. He'd humped his share of ladies, then he'd settled down and tried marriage. Tried twice to live with a woman and sire kids. But each time the woman had failed him.

The first wife had just given up. After eleven childless years, she had quit trying, and died along with his cattle the winter of the second freeze. The next wife was a quitter. She had fought alongside him through two years out beyond the Rincons, and then quit, taking her few possessions and slipping away.

Perce had no tolerance for women. If they didn't produce, like his horses and cattle, then they were useless. Easier to hire a houseboy, and ride to town when the urge got to him. It was a lot less bother than being wedded to one woman.

The two sisters were his problem now. Just the two of them working that ranch, no kids, no husband, just that plain-faced one who told him no so very politely, and the curvy one who turned her big eyes away from his glance. It would be a pleasure to move them out.

Perce wiped a broad hand across his face, feeling as he always did the extra tick as the stub end of that one finger bumped across his nose. By god, that was

57

almost thirty-five years ago he lost that tip. Down here in the Colorado foothills riding for the old man. He'd wrapped that finger tightly in a dally around the horn, too green to know you didn't tackle a fifteen-hundred-pound steer in the brush with a fast line. It had been his first drive, but old memories stayed with you.

Windy Dawes shoved his buckskin mare alongside Tolliver's black. The eager mare whickered an invitation; the stallion responded by stamping a forehoof and arching his neck, nickering back. Perce gigged the horse with a sharp spur to remind him of his manners. The two horses quieted down, and then stood still.

Perce spoke to his long-time foreman. His words were deliberate, his voice low and heavy:

"Windy, we got to move them women. I want them off their land, with no sign we had any part of it. I'm settling down here for good. Be here until I die. With no fight from th' law. Those days be over. There's a dance in town tomorrow night, and those two women will be there. I want you to check them there, make sure they be dancing, then burn their ranch. Set a good fire. But be careful, we want nothing pointing to us."

Windy Dawes tucked his head down, chewed at his lip, and listened very closely as his boss spoke the word. Tomorrow night. A dance in town. A fire at the Stuart ranch. He could see the line of kerosene poured around the back of the house, along the barn foundation. There was no tug at his conscience. This was what the boss wanted, and he would carry out the orders.

But for now suppertime was coming up fast, and Windy Dawes wanted to get that damned ugly son settled and get nearer to his own food.

George Ridgway was extra careful of his bruises, extra careful to explain to his wife and his afternoon clients just what had happened to him. How he had been an innocent bystander when the blow surprised him and knocked him down. Fighting was something George left for the law to handle. He did not condone fighting, and wanted it well established that he had not been at fault. Settling differences was for the court, not for him.

Old Mister Raynor had not tried to help him up, or even thank him for taking the blow, for being the intermediary between the rancher and his ill-tempered grandson. The old man had only turned away to watch the grandson take a short walk into the Texas Star. It had looked to George that the old man tried to hide a smile, but it must have been the angle from where he sat, down on the rough boards. As far as he had been able to see, there was nothing to smile about at all.

Harlow Raynor was seventy-nine years old and dying. Afraid of dying. He did not mind the pain as much as not seeing his line go on. He was the end of the line. Or rather, his daughter had been the end, but now she was dead, and he was dying. It was the bastard grandson who would have to be the continuation.

Harlow had watched the stiff-backed son take that turn into the saloon, with the cold coins held loose in his hand, and had moved away from the mewling lawyer still plumped on his backside. He had a lot of thinking to do.

Now he sat in the darkened rented room, surrounded by a very few memories of years past. His head reached partway up the back of the stuffed chair he had brought in from the ranch when he had come here to die. His spine rested on the seat cushion; his knotted hands hung onto the arms as if the grip would keep him from sliding to the floor. Sitting in this manner eased the tearing going on in his belly, lessened the biting pain that would consume him.

The face of Ben Raynor appeared in front of the old man: a thinned-down face that, even with its tired lines and dark-hued stubble, held the faint glimpse of his beloved Ellie. The old man wiped a spotted hand across his eyes, pressed the lids shut with blunt fingers, and stayed behind the welcomed darkness.

He could easily recall the tough look to his grandson, the quiet containment in the wiry body, the distant set to the pale eyes. And that fire-dark hair. He thought of Ellie's soft blondness, of Netta's yellow braid, of his own faded and lank brown hair now turned yellow-white.

Where had the boy come from? The old man shied away from the copper hair, the disturbing memories of his shadowed birth. He never had known who the man had been. Ellie had refused to say. And Netta could not stand the shame. Now the boy was all that was left.

It would have to be the grandson. He looked to have

the guts to bring the ranch back, to stock it and fight to keep the springs. For old man Raynor knew Perce Tolliver, knew him from the years behind him. Knew him as a wild youngster with a driving ambition that saw no man's interest but his own. A man greedy and without compassion. If Tolliver settled here in this wide basin, had bought his way in and was moving a herd into the hills, then Perce Tolliver wanted more. Wanted it all.

The answer was in the grandson. If the boy was as mean as his grandpa, then the same urges would bring him back home. Give the bastard the ranch over his outright refusal. Ignore the noise and hand him a signed and sealed deed. Get that soft-bellied lawyer to write up something nice and legal. Today. Before that youngster got too far away. From the set of his face when he'd lifted those rolling coins, he'd have to sleep off a good-sized drunk before traveling on.

The old man smiled, his seamed face twisting from the effort. He pounded with unexpected strength on the floor with his cane. The desk clerk down the hall knew the sound. The old man wanted something, and he wanted it right now. The clerk shoved a few papers into a ragged pile, and started walking down the long hallway.

George Ridgeway was surprised by the message that had been delivered by a small boy. After all the fuss of the morning, the curses and names called, Mister Raynor was going to hand over his property and cash to that sneaky son who said he was Ellie Raynor's only child. George bit his lip in small-boy

61

chagrin at his lack of charity and thoughts of foul language. The whole affair was his business only in carrying out the client's wishes to the extent of the law. Harlow Raynor wanted to hand over his ranch to a crazy man. Well, so be it. George sat back down in the oak chair and pulled the inkwell closer. He could be done with this and back home in a short while.

Part of Cable Orton's job in the town of Gladstone was to serve its legal papers, summonses, warrants, legal notifications. He wasn't too surprised when the lawyer entered his office, but did grin to himself as the man took his usual extended time explaining what the papers were about. When he had heard enough, Cable broke into the tirade:

"I do believe I know where this one went, Mr. Ridgeway. Sent him on his way out of town 'bout four hours ago. Heard too that he and his horse parted company not too much later. So he ain't gone far. You sure you want me to bring him back into this town, just to give him some papers? He might take it in his head to give you another punch. I'd stay out of his way if'n I was you. Dangerous life for a law fellow like yourself."

George knew the pattern of the marshal; The hulking man took a wicked, gleeful delight in teasing him. He would keep away from the man claiming Harlow Raynor as his grandfather. George ducked his head at the marshal as the big man finished writing out the receipt for the papers and passed it over his desk. He had had enough of this day. He was going to put up the "Closed" sign over his law office door and go home to Nancy. She would bring him back together and scatter the day's painful events.

Harlow Raynor watched as the shadows lengthened across the small room. Small, yes, but big enough to die in. He wanted to get up out of this damn chair, he wanted out of this room. Two feeble bangs with the cane brought no results. Harlow Raynor's deep sigh ended with a brittle cough that brought the pain back to his belly. Lighter this time, but still there. He had taken a good dose of the laudanum that Doc Halderson had left. It helped some, but it deadened his whole body, slowed down his mind. All he had left now were thoughts and memories, and he wasn't going to lose those with the medicine. The shadows reaching for him from the window grew stronger. Harlow thought of his grandson and grew quiet. He willed himself to wait, knowing he had put something wild in motion.

Strong fingers soothed round and round over George's damp forehead. Nancy knew exactly how to ease the tension. She hadn't laughed when he told of the meeting with young Raynor, the chase on the sidewalk, the unsuspected punch and humiliating fall. Nancy knew him well, knew how hard he tried to make things right in this young Colorado town.

The monotonous circles she drew on his brow eased away the upset. The baby was quiet; the darkness brought its own peace. Then she moved away from behind him and went quietly into the kitchen to begin his supper.

In the small room hung off the barn, Ben Raynor slept heavily, occasionally groaning deep in his sleep when an ill-timed urge to roll over punished his ribs. Fine drops of sweat covered his face, and the untreated cut, the size of sharp leather boot toe, had reopened to leave rusted smudges on the ticked pillow and tracks of blood through the moisture on his face. Exhaustion held him strong as he lay asleep on the loose-strung cot.

Up at the small ranch house; Emily Chapman absently poured another cup of coffee, forgetting to ask if Nora wanted one. She stared at the sewing in front of her, the bright-blue cloth almost colorless in the deep shadows thrown by a tilted oil lamp. Nora looked up from the ranch accounts, looked across the table at her sister. Emily caught the slight move and raised her head in answer. A meeting of eyes, a shared smile, and they went back to their work.

Nora found odd comfort in knowing that a battered, pale-eyed man slept outside in the shed. She shoved at her untidy hair, frowned in concentration, and erased one more number that had gotten in the wrong place. Bookwork be damned.

The knock startled them both, brought Emily hurriedly to the door. It swung open before she touched the tarnished latch. She stopped quickly, too close to Marshal Orton, whose large bulk took up the doorway, blocking the dark night outside. Emily stood close only for an instant, but it was long enough to breathe in the cleanness of the night, the smoky scent from the marshal. Her eyes widened as she almost touched his rough wool shirt.

The marshal looked down at the beautiful face in front of him, and gently moved to one side, breaking the unseen contact.

"Ladies, good evening." The marshal tipped his hat, then settled it back on his head. He wasn't here to be polite, but to deliver those papers to the drifter he had ousted not too long ago. He was gambling that the man was still here. He had heard Morse complaining in town.

"Miss Nora, you hire up a new man today? 'Bout so high, kinda thin, bunged up some, damndest fire-dark hair shot with white?" He smiled. " 'Pologize for the rudeness but I'm looking for such as him. Got a present from someone in town, something urgent they want delivered tonight."

Emily had gone to stand by her sister at the marshal's beginning words. She recognized in Nora the same instinct, that somehow they should defend the man asleep out in their shed. But from what she did not know. And this big bulky lawman did not seem to threaten the man, but wanted only to deliver a paper.

Emily put on a heavy wrap against the chill and took Cable Orton to the small shed. Nora sat back at her books, her mind wandering.

Emily returned alone, a long time later, something held tight in her left hand. Worry drew short deep lines around her mouth.

"We couldn't seem to wake him, Nora. The marshal even tried slapping him. He just mumbled at me and tried to hit Orton, but he never came fully awake.

Cable just grinned at him lying there, poked a few times at the bruises on his chest. And called him a poor son of a bitch. Didn't even try to apologize for this words."

She started out of the room toward the interior of the small house, then turned back to her sister.

"I'm going to take him one of Walt's old shirts and these infernal papers. Do you mind? His shirt is near to ribbons." Emily waited a moment, then continued in a low, concerned voice, "He is carrying a great deal of pain, and the marshal said it would get worse. You know, Nora, I think he was talking more about the papers than the fighting."

Chapter Six

He remembered voices during the night, something shaking him, poking him in the chest, the cot underneath him wobbling from the motion. Beyond that he had no memory, and as he came fully awake Ben Raynor struggled with the fragments, wondering if they were important.

Once awake, he wished he could have gone on sleeping. His ribs ached, the bruises pounded in his head in rhythm with his heartbeat. He could look down through the shredded shirt and see the dark flesh along his ribcage, and guessed the same color covered his back. Sometime during the restless night he must have scrubbed off the thin scabbing over his eye, and the stickiness on his check itched.

He sat up cautiously and looked around the small dark room. Piled neatly on the one broken-backed chair was a bulk of cloth with a white envelope tucked in a shirt pocket. He walked over slowly and reached carefully for the package, his entire body warning him to take it slow. By squinting he could make out the words on the folded paper: *These were left last night by Marshal Orton. Unable to wake you then.*

Thought you could use a clean shirt and razor. Breakfast is ready.

When he forced the rough-edged door open, Ben was surprised at the brightness of the day. The women would be up and about their work. A vague guilt nagged at him. Papers from the law meant nothing good. And how did the man know he was out here? Ben put the thick envelope back on the chair; those papers would wait until later. Right now he could see a wash basin and towel waiting by the back door. A shave and a clean shirt would start the day better than legal papers.

Stripped to the waist, his old shirt hanging by a torn sleeve, Ben hung up a stropping leather from a convenient nail and set about putting an edge on the rusted blade. Cold water would do, although he could see heated water, a curl of steam hovering over the top of a large pot sitting inside the kitchen door on the big, black cookstove.

The sweet-smelling soap lathered quickly, and left a pleasant pine scent as he pulled at the rough beard. Someone's man had bought well; the blade held a good edge once the rust was worked off it. Rinsing took some time, and left behind a lingering and unpleasant tingle. From the pink traces in the rinse water and the throb above his eye, he knew that cut had opened again.

"I can help you with that."

The gentle voice stopped Ben's hands as they held the towel over his face. He stayed in the rough darkness for a moment longer, using its safety to gather himself. Then he lowered the towel and faced the sound.

Emily Chapman was standing near him on the top step, a threaded needle and a small bottle in one hand. Concern showed in her eyes, concern and something close to pity. Ben accepted the offer with a short nod, and stood quietly as she reached to his face and prodded at the white flesh showing through the dots of blood above his eye.

Once or twice she started to speak, but a sideways glance at the grim face just under her hands stopped the impulse. Only involuntary twitches as the heated needle tugged at the open wound gave any indication that Ben Raynor felt what she was doing.

"Thank you, ma'am."

Ben knew his manners. He reached for Walt's old shirt and slipped it on. Nora Stuart had joined her sister at the door, and he was uncomfortable with the two women staring at him. The shirt was snug across his back, the sleeves too long, the fabric ballooning out in front of him.

"What do you want me doing?"

This was directed to Nora. Watching the color return slowly to the dark burned face, she outlined the day's work.

"We need to get the mares settled inside the barn. I want those big stalls cleaned out real good and deep bedded. Raynor, that's yours. Em, we need to bring in Duke and the rest of the band. Want to sort out the young stuff and start working them. Catch up Blue and Shorty. We should be back midday or later."

Nora smiled at her sister. "We can finish the home chores and get ready for the dance tonight." She turned back to Ben. "Once the stalls are done, go check the herd below. Make sure they're still in the valley. We block off the end, pile it with brush and deadfalls, but it always needs to be checked. You'll find the trail easy: go out to the road, turn right, and then left through the rocks. Take the bald-faced brown. He's easy to ride and knows the work."

She grinned slightly at Ben, to let him know she did not doubt his abilities, that it was his ribs she was babying, not him. Ben accepted the offer and turned to start the mucking-out. Emily slipped back into the kitchen as Nora called after their new hand, "Best come back and have a breakfast. Just a quick bite. Otherwise you'll have to wait till supper. It'll be a long wait."

Nora had a soft spot for the blue dun gelding. Walt had taken special notice of the horse as a two-year-old, and had spent extra time working with the animal, taking the patience to create a real working horse, one who moved by knee pressure and could carry a Spanish curb in a velvet mouth. She had watched Walt work the horse, and after his death she had continued the training. Now the blue was a special pleasure to ride, and, heading out to bring in the herd, she was extra glad to be mounted on a good horse.

It was Emily's voice that broke the quiet on the mountain trail:

"Did you see his back? Those big areas of shiny skin? I've seen that before, Nora. Fire. He's got another mark on his neck, and a long line across his chest, as if something had burned through him."

Emily shuddered at the picture her words made. It

was the worst kind of pain she could imagine. She glanced up at Nora, who had made no comment. Her sister's face held a peaceful set to the eyes, and a slight smile eased her mouth.

"You love it up here, don't you?" Emily asked.

"I'm me up here, not Walt's widow or that young woman who runs the Stuart place. The blue feels the same freedom I do." A more somber look replaced the pleasure on Nora's face as she continued, "Don't get to feeling sorry for Mister Raynor's grandson, Em. By now he must have read those papers. I'm betting they have to do with the R Cross. And we know Mister Raynor won't make anything easy for this grandson of his. We can't get involved. He'll be gone by tomorrow anyway. The papers will see to that."

The two horses walked on, the appy moving up to walk with the blue. Nora shifted in the saddle, then spoke again.

"I did see the scars. He's suffered all right. But from the look in his eyes, he won't say anything. He's going to hold on to that pain and let it eat him. Em, be careful. Stay away from him. There is nothing to him but more pain."

Nora urged the blue dun into a steady lope, impatient now to round up Duke and bring the rest of the herd home. The words had destroyed her magic time on the mountain. Emily followed her sister. The appaloosa's short stride became choppy as the horse struggled to keep up with the blue.

As she swayed with the quick strides, Emily let her mind go back to the pale-eyed man down at the ranch. Beyond the scars she had seen a strength, an economy of motion that spoke of ability and control.

71

Her breathing quickened, her heart pounded loudly; she could hear it above the clattering of the horses. She knew the signs: She had been alone too long. The dance tonight would give her a chance to play, to flirt with everyone, singling out no one special. She thought again of Ben Raynor, of his obvious disinterest both in her and in Nora. Neither of them reached him, got beyond the distant eyes and indifferent words. But the old man would keep him around, long enough for her to know him.

Emily smiled to herself, and Nora, turning back in the high saddle, saw her sister's face and was pleased. She put the blue into a run, and the appy leaped forward to catch up.

Bedding the stalls had been tedious work. Hauling the old straw out beyond the corrals, shaking down clean bedding and banking the stalls high along the outside walls took time and pulled at stiff, unwilling muscles. But Ben could understand the need for this work. The five mares stood quietly in their corral, head to tail, working against the flies. No need to get them this far with their babies and then lose them when the mares dropped an early-morning foal. These were older mares, well in their teens, proven mares who would carry worthwhile foals. The stalls would be their protection.

The brown gelding was easily fourteen years old, past prime for ranch work, but still a willing ride. Once mounted and on the trail, Ben could appreciate Nora's insistence that he take this particular horse. A long smooth trot that covered ground without jarring his body, an easy mouth, and no hint of a buck.

He wondered briefly about the gray, about his meager possessions. Shredded somewhere up in the mountains, strewn along a trail, ground into the dirt. With a jolt he realized that he had put the old man's papers down in the lean-to and hadn't gone back to read them. He settled back in the saddle. They would wait.

The ride to the long valley took less time than he had thought it would and he stopped several times at the wire fence to admire the small herd. The work was at the far end of the valley, where brush was jammed in the narrow neck of a short pass. The close-cropped grass and gentle slope tempted Ben, so he put the brown into an easy run. The horse and rider came up quickly to the valley neck, both blowing some and winded, but with clear heads. The brush pile needed shoring up, and the brown was cooperative in pulling over two deadfalls. Ben then cut some aspen, which he wove into the rotting mass that effectively blocked off the valley.

The creek running through the small graze was holding, but its trickle would dry up soon, and then the herd would have to be moved to higher range with constant water. Ben had heard Nora speak of the small spring high up behind the house. Her husband had had a good eye to settle this piece of graze. He walked the brown back along the thin trail that wound through the bright valley back to the ranch yard. Both he and the horse were pleasantly tired from their work.

He could see the horse herd coming in well before any animals were visible. They raised a considerable dust cloud, and the geldings in the smaller pen showed signs of excitement, tails lifting, nostrils flared wide. He had left the brown saddled, had only slipped the bit for the old timer to enjoy a well-earned nosebag of oats while he put together a lunch for himself. He had been surprised at his hunger.

It was impossible to get any sense of the size of the herd that Nora and Emily brought in. The women were dun-colored shapes as they waved their arms and shouted, maneuvering the dusty horses into the large pen. Ben roped the gate open, then stepped the brown backward, keeping a light tension on the rope looped around the gate.

Nora read his intentions, and grinned with appreciation as she rode from the corral. Then Ben gigged the brown forward as he smoothly coiled the line in his hand, pulling the gate hard shut behind him. A shift of weight brought the brown to a quick stop, and a knee turned him around. Pleased with themselves, horse and rider jogged up to face the boss.

"That was pretty cute, mister." A smile softened the ring to Nora's words. Then she started questioning him about the valley, the condition of the grass, the water flow, the shape of the herd. Emily took the blue's head as Nora stepped from the off-side to the back-door steps.

Nora called to Ben over her shoulder: "Give Em the brown and come with me. I need to talk over some things."

Surprise showed in Ben's eyes, but only for an instant. This woman was giving to him, treating him as an equal. He handed Emily the brown and followed Nora inside the kitchen. Nora continued her questions, listening intently as he spoke.

"It's the strangest thing . . ." Emily slapped at the dust ineffectively as she came through the back door, talking without looking. "We found a stray with the herd. Still saddled, but no bridle. Had a bosal on him tied back to the rig. A weasely little mustang scrub, flea-bit and nasty. Once I got a rope on him, he settled enough for us to go over him. I went through the gear. The owner sure didn't have much: a shirt, some dented cooking gear, and a wedding ring wrapped in a small bag. Not much else but worn-out clothes."

Emily stopped her chatter, suddenly very aware of a charge of feeling in the big room. Nora had watched the effect her sister's careless words had had on their hired man. The pale blue eyes had livened at telling of the grey's capture, then deadened at the blow-by-blow listing of what little they found in the saddle roll.

Then his mouth had tightened to a white line, and the small muscles along his jaw jumped and bunched as she talked on about the thin gold band carefully bound in a soft leather bag.

She watched in shock as Ben fought to bring clenched hands slowly away from the table where he sat. His body shook with an effort not to strike out at the beautiful woman who had just listed with callous indifference the entire contents of his life. The set to his face and the pain clouding his eyes drew her breath in sharp bursts.

For Nora had recognized the small gray once Emily had gotten a rope on him. She remembered the horse from the tie rail outside the Texas Star, and the man who had staggered out of the saloon at noontime, drunk and covered with blood. The same man who

75

had shown up on foot at their ranch, who had been hired as much out of pity as need.

She knew a good deal about this man, old Mr. Raynor's grandson—Ellie Raynor's bastard son born years ago and come home. But he had sat with them and shared supper, used Walt's favorite razor and donned one of his shirts, yet still gave them nothing of the man he was. She had only wanted to see something shake his calm sureness, put an emotion in the indifferent eyes. But not this much pain.

His hand trembled as he gently took the small soft pouch from Emily's open fist. Face blanched, shoulders shaking against the tension, their new hired man walked in careful, measured steps out the door leading from the kitchen and down the back steps, headed blindly to the small dark room leaning off of the barn.

The picture was there, still in his jumper pocket where he had put it yesterday. Safe. The ranch yard was quiet, the air still, as he walked. His feet raised small puffs of dust at each step. His hand clenched involuntarily around the smooth softness of the pouch, until the nails dug deep into his palm.

Behind him, in the kitchen, the two women searched each other's face, each full of unasked questions. A plate of sliced bread, cold beef, and a hunk of cheese salt waiting on the counter. Their lunch.

Chapter Seven

An hour after he left the kitchen, Ben was in the holding pen, rope in hand, watching the wily gray circle and dodge behind the other horses. The efforts kept him free until the flea-bitten gelding got too close to the bay stallion, who dropped his head and took a slashing run at the flank of the smaller horse. In his haste to escape, the gray ran into the small loop thrown by his former owner, and stood recaptured.

The saddle was unharmed, with only a few new scratches to add to the old collection. Loss of the bridle was a problem, but Ben remembered a broken headstall dumped in a corner, and there were several spare bits hanging on a wall. He backed away from the scrawny gray and shook his head. Owning this animal again was a dubious honor. Facing having to work from the gray made him appreciate the honesty and steadiness of the bald-faced brown.

Supper was another silent meal. Nora spoke once, to tell Ben that she wanted the team of roan mares hitched, that they were going to town for the dance. Emily kept her head down, careful to examine the food on her plate and avoid looking at Ben. She could still see the set to his face, the agony in his eyes, when he had so carefully lifted that small pouch from her hand. She could not look at him now.

Ben brought the team to the front door where the two women were waiting. Dressed in their best, they came down the steps together, faces flushed, eyes bright. Without speaking, Nora motioned for the reins. Ben hesitated, then past training that had been buried by recent years brought out the gentleman.

He bowed slightly to the women, held out his hand for Emily to assist her into the wagon. She was beautiful; the long, pale lavender dress, lace trimmed and demure, sculpted her body. It enhanced the vivid color of her eyes, the richness of her hair.

But tonight was Nora's turn. The blue dress, soft and flowing, fitted lightly to fall in easy folds, was a vibrant royal blue, the color bringing her face alive. Her eyes glowed; her hair, loosely curled and gathered at the nape of her neck, had already escaped the confinement, and tendrils curled along each ear, moving lightly across her breast, drawing the eye.

It was her eyes that dominated: wide, excited, lighting her strong features with a beauty that eclipsed Emily. Even as he put out his hand to assist her, Ben turned his head away. In the silence of the early evening, he watched the team pull out from the yard. For a short, painful moment he had wanted to join them, to take part in the laughter and promised pleasure of the evening. But he stepped back into the shadows. There was some harness mending he had to do.

Ben lay on the rope cot, tired from the long day, stiff and sore from the work and the beating. The patched and finished bridle lay on the floor beside him; the lantern had burned down to nothing. Hands locked behind his head, he let his mind wander. His eyes closed, and he drifted, halfway between memories and sleep. Then he slept, this time with no thrashing or sweated dreams. . . .

Whatever it was that brought Ben awake made him pull his mind together fast. Something was very wrong, something heavy, threatening, fearful. He sat up fast, searching his memory, uncertain if it was a nightmare that had brought him to the surface, or something outside.

Ben pulled on a jacket hanging from the nail and pushed the tight-fitting door open. Memory kept tugging at him, annoying him with its impatience. It probably was the mares, one starting to foal and having troubles.

The mares were fine; they ignored the shining lantern brought inside their stalls to check, and only blinked their eyes rapidly and turned their heads away from its irritation. They were all down, to ease the strain of the extra load. When Ben stopped at the last stall, he could smell what was wrong. Smoke.

Sweat instantly covered his face. He knew too well what smoke meant. He ran through the open back door and stopped abruptly. Low flames were coming up from behind the ranch house, barely visible flames, baby flames eager and deadly, rapidly growing larger. Grabbing a blanket from inside the barn, Ben ran behind the house where the flames were spreading out along the base of the wall. He flailed at the bright tongues, killing the ones in front of him only to watch the eager line grow longer further on, racing away from him as if following a trail. This fire was no fluke, it had been set—just like the other one that had taken his life.

Ben stumbled in his haste to bury the flames, cracked his head hard on a beam end jutting from the low roofline. Dazed, he worked harder in the battle to suffocate the fire with the heavy wool blanket. He was winning. The last seeking monster went out under his bootheel, and he leaned up against the warmed wall. A quick glance back to the barn showed him a new horror. The far side was too bright, highlighted by an eerie yellow glow. The barn was burning, the mares inside were helpless.

The big door resisted him, refused to open easily. Ben leaned back and yanked hard; the quick draft of fresh air through the center fed the flames, fanning their growth. Ben forced himself to go inside, but as the violent heat touched his face, a wavering picture of a woman screaming while her body cooked and of the weakened cries of a small boy stopped him. The nightmare was real again. Ben backed outside, drawing deep gulps of cool air into his lungs, battling the overwhelming fear, the paralyzing shame. He could not face this again.

Sharp memories seared him: the awesome pain, the rank, sweet smell of his own flesh burning, the twisted face of his wife, the blackened lump of his mother and his son burned together. He could not move.

A wild-pitched scream from inside the barn brought him back. A harsh scream of terror. The horses. The life of the ranch. The old mare in the stall near the front screamed again in agony as a burning wad of hay landed on her broad rump. The sound brought Ben back into the fight.

Grabbing his old faded saddle blanket and a broken rein from a pile, he jerked open the stall door and took a moment to croon softly to the frantic mare. His voice stopped the heedless circling just long enough for him to slip the leather around her neck and tie the wool blanket over her eyes. One tug on the leather strap, and the old mare calmly followed her guide, years of trust in man her savior taking over.

Turned loose in the yard, the mare trotted heavily to the large pen and stood by the gate, swinging around so she could keep a wary eye on the yellow monster. The band of mares edged close to her next to the fence, and together they watched the growing fire.

Inside the barn, Ben went to the next stall, the mare inside wild in her terror, screaming and circling her burning cell. But this mare, the youngest and wildest of the five, reared and struck out at the dim figure approaching her. An unshod hoof caught Ben high on his forehead, knocking him to the smoldering straw.

He rolled from the stall, more by instinct than from conscious thought. Head pounding, eyes blurred by smoke and blood, he left the stall open in the vague hope that the mare would find her own way to freedom, and staggered to the next stall.

This mare, older and wiser, let the gentle voice soothe her, allowed the leather strap to circle her neck, and sighed with relief as the warmed wool covered her head and shut out the horror. She trotted to her old friends in the yard, to stand at the corral fence with the band. Wiping his eyes clear, Ben went back in one more time.

Now the fire burned high overhead, consuming the loft of hay; the back door was rimmed with flame. The last two mares stood trembling at their doors, whickering to each other. Sisters, together for almost sixteen years, they waited now for Ben to rescue them. The red mare was dam of the good blue dun, sister to the rugged bald-faced brown.

The flesh of Ben's hand sizzled as he jammed open the stall latch, and the burning smell brought back the vivid memories, but only for an instant. The old mare nudged at him, eager for his rescue. She just needed the leather around her neck to convince her to leave the burning stall. She pulled Ben with her, and then stopped at the blazing door where her sister stood. The panel cracked and broke under the weight of the heavy mare's chest, and the younger mare followed.

Barely conscious, struggling with the burning air in his lungs, Ben could feel the old mare stop. Her body trembled underneath his arm thrown over her back for support. He hung from her neck, his feet dragging on the barn floor. He was depending on the old mare to bring them out of the flaming hell to the cool air just beyond the wall of the fire that had been the door. But the old mare refused to move.

Ben could only struggle to keep his feet; he tried to urge the mare on with his voice, but the flames heated his throat and left only a wordless croak. He knew his shirt was smoldering, that the mare's hide was burning, that a hot brand had been laid across his back; he knew the fire was there but he could not move enough to brush it away.

And still the old mare refused to move, only nickering sadly for the sister standing behind her. The roof peak broke in a shrieking cry and dropped flaming brands to the aisle below. The younger mare screamed her agony and lunged forward, knocking her sister staggering in a wild plunge through the flame-circled doorway.

Ben slipped beneath the big broken hooves, but instinct kept his hand tight on the leather rein. The old mare followed her sister's blind plunge, dragging the barely conscious man through the fire to the cool air outside and the comfort of the other horses.

Ben's hand was bound tightly in the leather strap holding him against the mare's warm body. But the constant strain on the dry leather and the multitude of small burns along its surface broke the line and dropped his soot-blackened body to the dirt floor beneath the protective feet of the burn-scarred mares. Inside the barn, one agonizing scream marked the death of the wild young mare. Then all was silent except for the settling cracks of the destroyed barn.

Chapter Eight

Eyes closed lightly, body swaying against her partner's arms, Nora Stuart leaned into the gentle tension at her waist and danced. She had danced every dance, waltz or square dance, each with a different partner.

A deep voice near her spoke insistently, demanding her participation. It was her partner, repeating a question. Nora opened her eyes and smiled most politely at the face near hers. Perce Tolliver. Talking to her, explaining something important. She listened to his sounds, admired their resonance, enjoyed their rhythm. Periodically she smiled at the older man, to let him know she understood, that she agreed with what he was saying. He was a good neighbor, an awkward dancer.

"*Fire.*" The word tore through the dancing pairs, stirred the onlookers along the wall, instantly brought the music to a dissonant and abrupt end.

"Fire. Out in the hills, near the Stuart ranch."

Men turned to Walt Stuart's widow and her sister, their faces flushed, bodies still moving unconsciously in the last steps of the dance. Nora turned pale; she grabbed Emily and ran for the door, the dancers on either side giving way to her rush. Women searched for wraps, picked out their young children, yelled for the older ones.

Buggies filled quickly, the men doubling up, the women taking the children home, already portioning out how they would get coffee and bandages to the scene. One man drove a team recklessly down the main street, heading to the Emporium shining bright with its new paint.

Arnold Hiller hurriedly unlocked his store, then went straight to the pile of new buckets. Grabbing as many as he could, he made several trips back to the buggy before satisfied he had enough. Then, forgetting to relock the store, he laid the whip to the morgan mare and she plunged into the collar, hitting a full gallop in three strides. He didn't let up until he reached the caravan at the edge of town.

Nancy Ridgeway stopped her husband before he joined the flight to the hills: "Someone will need to get the doctor. George, you take our team; I'll go with Heda Lautenclaus; she can keep William with her children and I'll come on to the fire. Quick, hurry. . . ."

The roan mares strained against the weight of the wagon, lashed into a frenzy by the harsh whip. They skidded around the corners, taking the stretches to the ranch flat-out. The light was stronger, the air hot and heavy. Emily held to the edge of the seat and alternated between watching Nora's face as she urged the mares, and glancing at the orange sky.

Fear rose in her: fear for the home she loved, fear for the horses trapped in the barn, and a horror that shocked her when she thought of the new hired man, left alone at the ranch, his body already carrying the shiny scars from another fire.

The mares had barely come to a bucking, sliding stop when Nora jumped from the swaying wagon seat and ran close to the flickering skeleton that had been their barn. Flames still rose from the pile of ash and charcoal that had once held her stock. She saw the mares huddled together by the big holding pen; a quick count and she knew one was missing.

All that came to her mind now was the new man: he must have freed the mares; they wouldn't have gone through the flames on their own. Her thoughts drove her frantic. Where was he? Her eyes searched the brightness of the yard, but she could not see the limp body hidden beneath restless feet.

Emily came closer to her sister and put her arm around the tense, drawn-up shoulders. They stood and watched the last upright fall in a tower of flame to land on the tilted doorway, bringing the few remaining timbers down in a vibrant shower. Two of the loose mares shied at the flare and broke into a ponderous trot across the yard to join the team. Lather had dried on the roans' necks almost instantly, covering them with a white rime of salt.

Wagons, buggies, a few horsemen, piled into the yard, sending the choking dust flying, obscuring the still form by the fence railings. Emily went with Nora to the back of the house, eager to check for more damage. Some of the men set up a bucket chain with the shiny new buckets to dampen down any escaping sparks. Others hurried to catch up with the sisters as they turned the corner, worried that the fire might have spread out of sight.

The effort needed to raise his hand those six inches, to lift it that high and wrap it around the bottom railing, took almost everything left in Ben Raynor. Bile rose in his throat, scalding singed tissue, echoing the deep flare of pain along his shoulder and in his hands. His eyes were glued shut by a paste of blood and ash mixed with corral dust. But his hand found the roughened wood and clung tightly to it.

The very slow movement interested a suckling foal, already bored with the commotion beyond the fence. Intrigued, he reached out his baby soft nose and snuffled at the warm sweet smell. The feather-light muzzle rubbed a fiery spot along the upraised arm, which jerked back from the contact and lost its hold on the rail. Ben flopped back to the dust and lay still.

The sudden fall sent the suckling backward in alarm. His dam, ready to spook from the excitement, whickered nervously and trotted away from the fence, head high in terror. The herd picked up her signal, and began to race wildly in the high-walled corral. The old sisters, standing over Ben, were caught up in the panic and trotted away in distress.

He had to try again. He had to get out of the dust. His lungs were living fire; the dust and soot were choking him. But the effort needed to get his hand back on the railing so close to his head was beyond him this time. His body hunched with a last feeble effort, then all the air rushed from his damaged lungs, and Ben Raynor collapsed back into the killing dirt.

Coming back around the far side of the house, Nora saw that the mares were now standing by the team, that the penned herd was racing blindly. She saw the brief convulsion of a dark shape. Running wildly, pushing people away from in front of her, she reached the fence and knelt in the dust. One trembling hand reached out in awe to touch the charred body at her feet.

Her voice was a soft rasping whisper: "Oh no. Oh my god, no." Charcoaled fingers moved spasmodically in the dirt. Ben heard her hushed words, felt her gentle touch. His head raised a short distance from the ground, then flopped back from the effort.

"Quick, help. He's alive."

People ran to the words; the doctor reached the two figures first. Practiced hands lightly touched Ben's face, lifted an eyelid to peer at disappearing eyes.

"He is alive, all right. Barely. Emily, you and Nora get a bed ready in the house. Someone get a lantern. Get a door and lots of blankets; it'll be easier to move him. Hurry."

Ben was aware of the words, could hear the scuffling around him. But his mind was centered on the raging pain that held him, a familiar pain that he knew would never leave. A small flame reached through his shocked mind and triggered a spasm of fear, shaking his body and giving him the strength to strike at the glow.

Doc Halderson saw the rising panic in the injured man, and quickly realized he was fighting the lantern flame held too close to his face. He waved the lantern away, and Ben's arched body slumped back to the ground.

By careful stages they rolled Ben onto the door and carried the improvised litter to the house. At the doctor's insistence, everyone except the sisters left the room. Outside in the yard, food and coffee had arrived. The men went back to their bucket chain to wet down the embers, and others began the tedious chore of cleaning up.

Doc Halderson's hands were large, with long fingers and heavy flat knuckles. Hands of a farmer, strong working hands that broke delicate things easily. Yet hands that gently peeled back the remains of Walt Stuart's shirt from the blackened body. Hands that picked out the smallest remnant of fabric, plucking the tiniest bits from the burned flesh.

Infection would set in wherever foreign bodies remained. Infection would kill the already weakened man. In his deep concentration, the doctor groaned aloud as he examined a burn that was raw and wide open; there was no similar response from the patient. The pale eyes were open, flickering whenever Halderson touched the warmed flesh, but the man behind them seemed to be deep inside, separate from the pain. Not unconscious, but immune to what had to be agony.

It took the doctor much longer to assess the damage to his patient than it took the town to kill the remaining embers and pen up the pregnant mares. One man volunteered to stay the rest of the night; Nora tiredly accepted his offer, and showed him where he could bed. It left one less thing for her to worry over until morning.

She walked back to the house slowly, knowing that the doctor would be done soon, and be able to tell them what the chances were. Her steps slowed as she neared the house. Emily had stayed to work with the doctor, laboring over the mute form, peeling back destroyed tissue, cleaning the open sores, layering them with lard and clean cloths. Only once, when the doctor and Emily had picked ash and gravel from the deep burn across his back, had Ben fought them, pushing up from the bed on bandaged hands, fighting their soft restraint. The doctor had dripped a small amount of chloroform through a loose cloth over his nose, careful not to touch the singed flesh.

"Nora"—the doctor's voice brought her the rest of the way up the steps to the large living room—"The burns are not as bad as we first thought. Mostly superficial, only the one across his back is really deep. It is his lungs that worry me. How badly they are damaged we won't know, but I know they are not good. If there are complications it will be his lungs. I'm sorry."

It had to be a nightmare. Voices talking over him, hands reaching down to him, pulling at his flesh, touching his forehead. Eyes peering at him, disembodied eyes with nothing behind them. And the screams. From his memory. They had to be. The screams could not be him. Animal screams rising to high pitch, cut off sharp and clean. Human screams that tore at him, begged him, cursed him. Screams that never ceased.

Something sat heavy on his chest. It kept him from getting the cool, healing air he needed to ease his starving lungs. It was crushing him, taking the air away from him, drowning him in a heavy liquid that stole his strength. And the hand that kept after him. Hands that were always there, that kept him from tearing the rigid bands that covered him, that held

91

him down. Hands that put ice-cold fire against his flesh, hands that drew blazing cold across his chest, taking what little breath he could manage, and freezing it inside him.

Sometimes the hands forced his lips apart, made him hold a running fire in his mouth that choked him, that blazed down his throat to burn deep. Then all the pain went away, and he could rest.

For a while. Until it all started again: the fever, the burning deep in his body that no icy cold could reach, the fire across his back and shoulder, the pounding in his head that threatened to split him apart.

Always hands. Sometimes voices, often eyes, but always hands. And he cursed in a silent voice that he was too weak to fight them. . . .

Ben found that if he worked hard, if he thought about the motions that were needed, the multitude of moves he had to make, then he could, very slowly, roll his head to one side and open his eyes. It took all his strength, but he could do it. The light from a low-trimmed lamp was nearby, a friendly flame, just enough for him to see the woman asleep in the big chair near his bed.

Only it couldn't be his bed. That had burned a long time ago. The thought drove a deep pain through him, and an involuntary cry came from him. The sound startled him. The woman in the chair stirred, wiped a blistered hand across her face and opened her eyes. It was Nora Stuart.

"Ben." The voice was soft, ragged, almost a whisper, as if she were afraid of him.

"Ben. You're awake." Such simple words, obvious words. Why did they bring tears to her. Before he could frame the question in his mind and find the words to speak, Ben Raynor slept.

Then it wasn't a struggle to open his eyes, and he could roll his head on the pillow with only a little effort. His breath was short, painful, but he could form words and makes sounds.

"Good morning. I hear you tried getting up this morning. Not yet my friend."

The words from the large doctor were an encouragement. "Not yet." Soon he would be up. Ben watched the doctor walk through the darkened room to the back of the house, to the kitchen where Nora and Emily were working. He lay on the old leather couch and listened to the hurried words spoken just out of his sight.

"He's through the worst. With more of your good care he will come back. Now he needs to build strength, regain muscle, exercise that arm and shoulder to restore what he can. It will be very painful, but he must get up in another week or so and make the effort. Otherwise he will be a cripple. It will be hard for you both. You will have to button his clothes, do small tasks that require the use of hands. His fingers haven't healed well enough to risk going without bandages. But he must get up and walk outside—to the barn, to the backhouse—every day. But be careful, or his lungs will reinfect."

Nora nodded her understanding of what the doctor was saying. There was more pain ahead but Ben had come through the worst. She returned to the big front room, the sick room, leaving Emily to deal with the care of the shoulder burn and the hands.

She found Ben sitting, with his legs over the edge of the old, worn couch. Sweat covered his gray face, showed in great circles under his arms and down his back through the light cotton nightshirt. He did not look up at her approach, but spoke to her with hoarse unsteady words.

"I heard. I know what the doc is talking about. I've been here before." Pain clouded the pale blue eyes, turning them a smoky gray.

He leaned forward to find his balance, spread his feet wide apart, and tried to stand. Nora put out a hand, the tips of her fingers just beyond his reach. Without looking up, he seized her fingers and pulled himself erect. She felt the trembling in the damp hand, looked down and saw the pale white feet braced far apart on the dark wooden floor. She heard the gasps as he fought for the first step. Inside her mind she cried, silent and alone, at the pain she felt coming from the man, but she looked at the grim face, intent on the execution of that first step, and she bit her lip to be still.

Ben took four steps and stopped; his hand gripped hers harder, crushing the fingers together, then the pressure relaxed and he toppled to the floor before she could reach him.

Then Emily was with her, violet eyes blazing. The doctor stayed in the doorway, watching the three people crouched on the floor. One on each side, the women knelt to bring the sick man back to his bed. Ben refused the help.

Face blanched white, body trembling in exhaustion, he shook off the supporting hands and struggled to sit up. There was nothing he could reach to pull himself erect. He would not lean on the women. The faded leather couch was out of his range, but so very close.

Pride buried in pain, body shaking, he pushed himself to his knees, tipped forward and landed heavily on outstretched hands. The pain came in waves through the heavy bandaging on his fingers, and drew his mouth to a thin line.

Slowly, carefully, caught in the voluminous folds of the nightshirt, Ben Raynor crawled to his bed.

Emily turned away from the man down on hands and knees. Nora put one hand over her mouth and took in a big gulp of air. The doctor, still watching from the doorway, smiled—a grim and bitter smile that saluted the creeping progress of his patient, lauded the man, as he struggled to raise himself enough to slide onto the cool leather surface of the couch.

Chapter Nine

The summer sun was unforgiving. Even hidden deep under the sheltering veranda roof, Ben could feel the hot wind coming down from the mountains behind the ranch house, raising dust in the yard as it blew out across the basin. The loose shirt he wore barely rested on his chest and shoulders, yet where it touched it stuck to the damp flesh beneath.

He tried leaning against the back of the chair. The draining sore across his shoulder sent its message and he winced from the reminding pain. He had gone beyond his goal for the day, and his still-weak flesh was reminding him of its frailty.

He was on the mend. His hands were no longer bound with strips of white rags; his hair had started regrowing, spiky and stiff with gray streaks scattered through the copper brightness. And his face no longer had a glossy redness from singed skin, but had faded to the pale gray of an invalid.

Since the morning he had crawled across the big room's floor, Ben had been up and walking. At first only a few steps, but each day had brought more steps and longer distances. This morning he had walked to the shed, picked up a brush, and worked over the brown gelding. For that short half-hour he had been able to forget the pain of the past five weeks; he had closed his eyes to the smell of warm horse and the soft sounds of sweet hay being chewed. Now he was paying for that interlude. His eyes shut, he let his head rest lightly on the chair back, and dozed in the noontime heat.

Nora Stuart reined in the blue dun when she saw the slight figure rolled up in the chair. Unconsciously she glanced at the half-raised skeleton growing from the ashes of the old barn. Tomorrow was Saturday, and a crew would be here from the neighboring ranches to finish the framing. The men had already sorted themselves according to their skills; the women had the food prepared. Tomorrow the shell would be finished.

She walked the dun to the shed where what equipment they had salvaged was hung on nails. The horror of the past weeks was still strong in her. The ever-present smell of ash stayed heavy in the summer sun, never relenting. And whenever she took a bath to scrub herself clean of the constant grit, she would find ash floating on the surface of the clean water.

Reminders were everywhere. But the worst of the memories were of the long nights with the patient. Horrible nights of suffering each breath with the unconscious man as he had struggled to bring clean air to damaged lungs. There were memories of the early hours, when even with the medicine the pain had been unbearable, and tears had slid down the shiny face from under gummy eyelids. And then there were the times when Nora had come to get her sister for breakfast, and she had found Emily in tears, rocking back and forth in the chair by the couch, in as much pain as the patient.

The dead mare. The dead mare had been uncovered in the ash and steaming wooden pyre on the second day. The hide had burned away to leave blackened flesh, with bone showing through, white and stark in its black surroundings. Two men had tried to move the pile, and the flesh had pulled away from bone. They had finally butchered the carcass and rolled it in pieces in a canvas tarp.

They had found the foal inside; complete and intact, protected by its mother's flesh in its own liquid cradle. A red bay colt, near term and perfect. Grim-faced and silent, the men had completed their chore, then mounted their horses in a hurry, eager to hit town and the Texas Star. . . .

And there had been the visitors. The ladies from town organized in relays to come out to the ranch and help each day with the invisible chores. One sat with the injured man, wiped his heated face with a cool cloth. The other would talk with Emily and Nora, bake bread, do anything to take some of the burden from the two women.

The marshal came, doffed his hat to Miss Emily, and asked to poke around in the remains. He walked through the smoldering ruins around the back of the house, stuck his fingers in the line of ash. He asked very few questions, for this was not his jurisdiction, but he'd been curious.

He came in to stand over the unconscious man on the wide leather couch. He stayed only a short time, and said very little, his face grim in the shadowed room.

The old man came to the ranch. On his first visit he pulled himself up the front steps, rested on the porch for a long while, refusing Emily's offer of a chair or some lemonade. He walked very slowly across the planked floor to the man lying so still under a light covering. The old man leaned heavily on his cane and looked down at the ravaged body, a torn sheet covering its gauntness, lumpy raised areas of thick bandaging visible through the almost-transparent cloth.

The old man's face did not soften as he inspected his grandson, but he had to have seen the evidence of great pain, the twisted edges of the sheet, the hot glaze to the unseeing eyes. The copper hair was badly singed, the grey streak showing stark along his temple. Eyebrows and lashes had been burned away, leaving the naked face a shiny parchment red.

With the second visit, the old man accepted Nora's arm to climb the steps and leaned heavily on the cane to walk the distance to the shadowed couch. This time the pale eyes were focused, could see the lined face of the old man. Mister Raynor asked about the papers. And the patient rolled his head away from the question, closed his eyes. His hand convulsed and knotted the sheet. Then the fingers opened, helpless even in that small effort. A bent and spotted hand reached out, then stayed in midair and returned to its position on the twisted silver-headed cane.

Old man Raynor stayed for a long time in the darkened room, sat for most of the afternoon in the heavy rocker and talked to the mute invalid. Nora walked him back down the steps. Once in his carriage he looked down at the young woman and smiled.

The steady black gelding brought the old cowman back to town, and pulled up in front of the gently swinging sign at the lawyer's office. George Ridgeway came out to help the old man inside.

"Lawyer, draw up those papers again. Give the boy the ranch. No strings. Just give it to him. Now, take me back to my room."

He poked George almost gently in the ribs with that ever-present cane and hobbled back to the waiting black, assuming that George would follow. In his room, he sank deep into his chair, dozed intermittently, and waited for the dark.

Perce Tolliver cursed Windy Dawes, railed against the ill-timed interference from a saddle bum, and took his opening. He became a concerned neighbor, sending men to do ranch chores, shipping over a haunch of beef, stopping by to smile at the women, to wish them well and probe for weakness. As a friend, he sent Lug Bremen and Mont Hackett to the valley graze to round up the small and precious herd and drive them to the high grass.

Ben awoke dazed and disoriented by the intensity of his short sleep. Nora's footsteps on the veranda steps brought him fully awake. He blinked his eyes shut and stayed quiet, letting her pass into the house without words. Hearing the footsteps recede into the kitchen, he opened his eyes again and began the struggle to sit up. Hunger brought him out of the chair and into the house.

Uncomfortable in the damp smelly shirt, he fumbled at the buttons, his fingers too tender to find a grip. He cursed his uselessness, and heard a soft laugh. A hand reached to him and took the front of his shirt, wadding it in a bunch. Then Emily Chapman pulled him slightly off balance, forcing him to take one step nearer to her. He leaned back against her demanding hand and twisted his shoulders. Her hand dropped away and the smile lingering around her mouth disappeared. A quiet sigh left her, then she brusquely unbuttoned the wet shirt and walked away from him. Her voice reached him from the doorway:

"Best eat lunch now; we're going to work stock this afternoon, be late coming in. The whole town will be here tomorrow for the barn-raising. You're the hero, you know."

Ben frowned at the words. He wanted nothing to do with this town, or any town. But the knot of hunger in his belly brought him to the big kitchen for the noon meal. He ate in silence, the sisters talking over him, working out the afternoon's chores.

He would be gone from here soon. To the R Cross, his ranch. He thought of the papers that had been delivered yesterday by one of Perce's men, sealed with an official waxen stamp, giving him the abandoned ranch further up in the hills. After tomorrow he would use the house to live in while he finished healing. Then he'd use the money to move on. He had to get away from the two women.

Only half taken with Emily's talk, Nora watched the bent copper head, damp hair loosely curled along the neck. The man still ate with awkward movement, the skin on his hands brittle and stiff, making it difficult to bend around a knife or fork. She saw the thin shirt rise and fall in a short, irregular pattern as he fought for breath.

Ben looked up from his plate and caught Nora's stare. He looked back down at the partially eaten food. She bit the corner of her lip in distraction. She had bathed this man, held him close, cried for his pain, listened to his fevered ramblings. She knew what had kept him so distant, knew who had belonged to the thin gold ring. But the pain, and the intimate knowledge, had not opened him or brought him closer.

She wanted something from him. She wanted what she had formed with Walt. But he only looked at her and looked away, giving nothing back. She had seen Em tease him, she had seen his stiff-necked refusal to play. The first fire had burned out the very core of the man, leaving nothing for her. Nora sighed and came back to the rattling dishes, and Em's smiling voice: "He's gone outside, Nora. We've got work to do."

Just after sunrise, the air still holding the nighttime chill, a wagon pulled into the ranch yard. Four riders followed, then a group of carriages from town. And then still more wagons, loaded with men carrying hammers, saws, boxes of nails lying between their feet on the wagonbeds. Fancy buggies came, bringing women and children from town, the floor space in these filled with food, plates of cakes, crocks of hot stew, pies still steaming. They were here to complete the barn.

Women poured out mugs of steaming coffee; men found their work stations and went straight to work. Children were everywhere, carrying tools, fetching more nails, chasing each other around, and forever drifting by the dessert table to tempt a pinch of frosting or a handful of filling.

The good feeling of the activity pulled at Ben. He had a special place with these people, though he did not want it. His few attempts to work alongside the men cutting boards or pounding nails met with smiles and conversation, easy voices and overtures of friendship. Wherever he went the work stopped for the moment. They thanked him, they wished him well, some even forgot and made to slap him on the back. But in all the talk and laughter, they did not let him cut a board or pick up a nail.

Long before noon he gave up trying. He found himself sitting on the wide veranda steps, tired from the morning yet having done nothing. Part of his mind registered the footsteps crossing the big room inside the house, heavy steps, carried in short, quickened strides. Then behind him he heard the front door open, close, and the steps stop just behind him. He did not make the effort to turn his head or question who was standing behind him.

Cable Orton's deep voice fitted the size of his steps, Ben nodded to himself. Orton sat and grunted with the effort. He watched the profile of the hunched man beside him, noted the tension in the wide mouth, the deep lines at the eyes. He was bemused by what he saw. For one who cared so little, this man's presence had changed a lot of lives in a short time. Yet beyond his actions, Orton knew he had read those pale blue eyes correctly. The man plain didn't want to give a damn.

The old man had been at him again in town, going

on about Perce Tolliver, the springs, and the good folk who would lose out. Orton had dismissed those notions as coming from an old man, as being not of town business, beyond his jurisdiction. But the fire, the shadow of suspicion that it had been set, ate at his confidence.

Something was moving in his town that he did not like. And somehow this stolid faced man was right in the middle of it. Old man Raynor had an itch in his craw about Tolliver. But his suspicions and mutterings had been nothing but fantasy until this fire.

Cable sat next to the white-shirted hero and watched the confusion spread before them. Men were everywhere, working, talking, drinking, wiping the sweat from their eyes. And out there were three hands come over from Tolliver's Traveling T. Supposed to be working. But one of them kept his gun strapped down, wouldn't hang it up to work. Cable didn't like that stamp of man around his town.

He glanced again at the man sitting beside him, so quiet, so distant. And looked again—there was something here he didn't believe. A hint of a grin working the quick mouth. He spoke fast to take the advantage:

"What be on your mind that's so damned funny? Ain't nothing fun 'bout having to rebuild a burned-out barn. Lots of folks out there working hard in this damned heat, and you and I just sitting here. With you grinning."

The answer was simple. And it was funny.

"Orton, you sent me packing from your town. Now you sit here and watch that same pure town work. Because of me. Kind of a turnaround."

His voice became serious, the wide mouth pulled

tight, the touch of humor left the pale eyes. "I know fire. This one was set. The old man is betting on Perce Tolliver. You know that. And I know it." Raynor looked at the yard of activity. "It's your town, you say. What are you going to do?"

Orton was mad. "If'n you know it was set, how come I don't know you set it?" The instant anger had put foolish words in his mouth. His companion only looked sideways at the big lawman.

"Okay, that was pure stupid," Orton admitted. "Maybe it is my town, but it's your ranch that's in the middle. Your ranch, the springs, and a big mess of hard questions if the old man is right. Got any plans?"

Orton felt rather than saw the reaction. The easy good humor was gone for good; the dead set to the pale eyes had returned, bringing back the hardcase he had kicked out of his town. Whatever interest their talk had uncovered, the spark was buried again under a distant gaze and an uncaring face. Cable found unreasoning anger build in himself against the man. Anger that fought with the growing like he had been nurturing. His words were harsh:

"Mister, do you ever care what a body says to you? Look, you got a ranch, two women who owe you, and an old man who has given you more than you deserve. And you sit there playing games with words and doing nothing. If I was you I'd get going. Do something with those words. Damn you, you ain't nothing but a late-cut gelding."

The oath brought a rush of words to Ben's mind, words that fought to be said. Words about the pain of caring, the futility of fighting for what was yours. He sat silent in the dusty air. The heartbeat moment when he could have connected with the bulky lawman passed. Time grew into a long minute.

Finally, Ben struggled wearily to his feet and looked down at the broad shoulders of the marshal.

"Orton, someone will do something. Only it won't be me."

He walked stone-faced through the throng of townspeople and ranchers crowding around the long tables set for the noon meal. Men tried to stop him, to offer lunch, words, friendship, but he looked through them and continued his line of march to the carriage shed. Inside there was a bed, away from the two women and the press of people. He settled painfully on the narrow cot and fought to wipe his mind blank of the past.

Chapter Ten

The black horse reared at the heavy hand on the bit, and Perce Tolliver put spur to the animal, punishing it hard. He steadied the stallion, then crossed his hands on the horn to watch Dawes and a new hand work the small herd of heifers into the pen with the eager bull.

It was the wrong time of year to be breeding stock, but he was impatient, and these blooded whores were barren. By the next winter he would have grass-cut hay stored and waiting and a barn that could hold expectant mother and late-summer calves. Better to get started now, than to leave the ladies empty until another season.

Tolliver gigged the black horse forward to angle up and meet with Dawes. He took absent note that the new hand, Blake Morse, when he knew the boss was watching, handled his horse better, had a more jaunty set to him. That vanity could be a tool. Perce didn't like the too-handsome Morse, but they needed another winter hand.

The two men met just outside the high-walled breeding pen. Windy spoke in his usual short bursts:

"By gawd there, Perce, that there son may be ugly, but he sure to hell know what he's for on this earth. He won't never be a tender meal for no one."

The bull was bellowing his challenge, snorting in lusty determination as he circled the bewildered cows. The season was wrong, the months coming too cold, but the instinct to reproduce was rampant in the bull, and his ardor awakened his court, brought them to lift their tails and stand for their suitor. The stubby legged, heavy muscled bull was well started in his contribution to Perce's fortune.

"Windy, we got to get at the Stuart girls' herd. Take three, four riders, ones you can trust, run off most of the herd we moved up to the springs. Isherton down by the border can take the cattle, pay you some, and lose them in his spread for the winter. But get rid of them cows fast. That little lady needs to know she's heading through the winter with nothing coming in the spring. That'll help her to appreciate my offer when I make it again. Take Morse there with you. He's likely enough."

Dawes sat his restless buckskin mare and watched the boss ride out. Stealing cattle from a widow didn't seem the way to settle in nice. But it was what Perce wanted, so he would do it. Morse reined in his roan next to Dawes's mare.

"Morse, you done here. Tomorrow we ride out real early. Be ready come light to travel, and travel fast. Going up to the mountains, to t'other side, and taking along a herd a cows. They got business down near the border."

Then Dawes swung the mare aside and loped her back to the ranch buildings. Tolliver's black whistled from his pen at the pretty buckskin as Morse sat on his roan and speculated on the high, thin back of the riding boss. Whatever was coming tomorrow, he'd made sure to be right there with it. This was a good berth: good horses, plenty of food, good pay. And a town close-by. Just had to keep his mouth shut and mind his business. Something more was going to come his way, give him a handle that would set him easy for life.

Blake Morse hadn't been born to work for the rest of his life in the dirt. Extra knowledge, something out of line that he could prove, and he would have Tolliver's balls right where he wanted them—in a vise between the law and Blake Morse. Given time he could come to see Tolliver as the pa he never knew. Given enough time and the right handle.

And somewhere along the line he would tend to the other business: Them two women who drove him off, and the saddle bum who had been there to witness his humiliation. His face winced at the bitter memory. That bum had gotten in the way of a fire, been living on his injuries ever since. Probably bedding down them two, living like a king. Morse grinned and his handsome features took on the lines of a scavenger. They better enjoy what they got now, for he was planning on some rearranging.

The idea hit Perce several days after Dawes had taken his crew up into the mountains on their "errand." He had been watching his bull mount another she-cow. A party, a real shindig—that's what he needed in this sober town: A party that would draw

111

the ranchers, bring them to his house, into his circle of power. Make them beholden to him.

The fall was a good time—late fall with the winter hay in, the cattle brought close to the home ranch. Time when folks were looking ahead at the long, dismal winter cold. Clean up his barn and throw a big one. Get the sisters to organize it. Get that pretty one to spend his money, make all his plans. Get the plain one to set the food, get them both to the ranch. Get them in his shadow. He grinned. The ladies would never know how big the debt was. As of now their cattle were beyond the mountain pass, on their way to a new brand and a short range.

Tolliver sat back in the rawhide chair and wrapped his hands in back of his neck. The Jackman buildings were barely enough to hold him. But they were a toehold in the basin. He brought the chair back hard to the floor and slapped the scarred desk. Now was his time, not in a few years, and never in the past. Now he would have it all, and damnation to anyone who got in his way.

Perce pushed aside the leather-backed chair and walked to the edge of the long veranda outside. One hand was in sight, leading a gimpy horse toward the corral. The urge to ride out came strong in him, and his voice crossed the yard in a roar, setting the roan back on the trailing lines.

"Get me a good horse, right now. My gear, and make sure there's a long gun in the boot. Goddammit, now."

His command raised the cowhand into an unaccustomed run, the roan pulling back in a ragged jump to the half-empty barn. When the boss spoke around here, by god, you answered in a two-step.

One hour later Perce hauled in a laboring chestnut and dropped the reins loose on the sweaty neck. The tired horse was grateful to stand, his sides heaving in deep bursts of air. Below were the old man's spring and the faded grass that were his riches. The squat rancher let a long sigh escape as he looked over the land before him. Gold got to some men, drove them feverish with a need to have. Women got to others, or horses. But for him it was land. Land like this: strong, wild, and promising everything to its taker. Land that would grow his cattle, land that lived with the clear bubbling spring set deep under the shadow of a mountain.

He knew there was another, smaller pool beyond the line of rock, belonging to the women. Perce snorted his disgust, and the harsh, unexpected sound spooked the half-broke chestnut. The gelding snaked his head down and to one side, found the reins swinging free and shook his heavy neck.

Perce swung his weight to grab the leather, but the horse evaded his control and plunged down the hillside, sidestepping the rubble, always tossing his head to evade Perce's hands. The rank gelding gathered speed, and by the time he hit the bottom he was running out of control, with Perce digging at the lathered sides to keep the horse's head up.

But the chestnut was too clever to be goaded. Down went the big roman head and the chestnut bellowed in his fury, sunk on his haunches then shot up and forward. Perce rode with the buck, gouging with each leap, embedding his spurs in bloodied flesh.

It was a short and violent battle, with only one

113

outcome possible. Without a hand on the bridle, Perce had nothing to set himself against. The bucks grew wilder, more pounding, but the man rode his damndest, spurring frantically. One more twisted leap and Tolliver slipped from the saddle to land hard on his shoulder, rolling free with the instinct of years. He sat up, fought for his breath, and watched the disappearing rump of the bucking chestnut head down the meadow, bending the lush wild grass under his feet. Tolliver cursed and stood up, found his hat, and remained for a long moment alone in the wild valley.

The bald-faced brown gelding labored to climb the precarious trail that led straight up into the hills. Ben Raynor leaned forward over the animal's withers and stood in the saddle to ease his weight from the horse's back. With a final lurch they reached a small rock plateau where Ben reined in the brown and waited for both of them to catch their breath.

Up this high he could turn back in the saddle and see for miles across the valleys, out onto the large basin that held Gladstone. Two weeks ago on the day he moved into the old man's ranch, he had listened to Nora Stuart describe the trail, calling it the old back way, the one to use in a hurry. Not the trail they used to move stock, but one for a fit and clever horse.

He was in a hurry. He wanted to test his fitness, find out how far he could push. The move to the R Cross had taken too much from him, and it had been four days before he saddled the brown and rode across the ranch.

The old man had willed him a glimpse of heaven.

114

High grazing land just waiting to be stocked. Graze that would carry a big herd, grow fat beeves, strong horses. Ice-cold water that would guarantee his survival, and his neighbors'. His ranch.

Ben had awakened early in the morning, driven by ghosts from the comfort of his roll spread by the back door. Something came at him hard, egged him to ride out and check the hills, to scout the range. An edge had come to him as the hot summer winds gave in to the coolness of fall. A decision was waiting for him: Ride out soon, or stay and take up what the old man had left him?

He swung the blown horse off the rock and followed the deep-gouged trail down a rock-covered incline, through a stand of bright yellow aspen in their fall colors. The old man's spring, his spring, should be coming up soon. The Stuart spring was another two miles back through a break in the steep hills. He wanted to see them both.

The swirling wind brought a touch of coolness with it, the tantalizing hint of water. The brown stopped short to spook at a small herd of deer, which fled at the sudden movement. Ben settled the horse and stepped down.

The spring was a miracle. A wide pool with many trails leading to its edge. Beyond lay a tumble of rock, jagged and rough, piled high from an old slide. At the center of the pool was a frothy white bubbling, the center of the spring. All this was his, even if he did not want it. Ben shook his head against the traitorous thoughts. He walked back to the brown, head down, refusing to look at the wide, lush graze and ever-flowing water.

At his touch the brown headed down the slope and across the empty land. Ben put the horse to a faded trail that headed toward the Stuart land. The rolling grasses gave way to a narrowed confusion of tree and fallen rock. One faint path led over the top of the small rise and another valley was exposed. Not so rich, so lush, as the land behind him, but enough for anyone.

Nora Stuart had spoken of her small herd of three hundred cattle, of Perce Tolliver's men driving them up here for the summer range. But to Ben's practiced eye there were less than fifty head in the valley. He put the brown to a run down the center of the graze, deliberately scattering the bland-faced beeves as he plunged through their middle. No more than fifty head at quick count. He turned the brown and watched the cattle spread out into the trees. Fifty would be a kind guess.

He went back to the spring. Head down, he eyed the small crisscrossed paths that led to the water, looking for some answer.

Several of the paths were covered with fresh droppings; they converged onto a main trail heading out of the high valley. The trail showed chopped edges from many hooves, muddied with tromped-down manure. The line followed a winding, brush-jammed climb over rocks to parallel a deep canyon that formed the northern boundary of the Stuart range. Ben sat for a moment on the uneasy brown and let his eye roam the land.

The brown swung around, ears pricked tight, spooked by something coming up behind him. Ben let the horse turn, and watched a rangy chestnut, head

high and reins trailing, come at a sideways lope to stop
hard and stick his nose out to just touch the brown.
Ben reached to pick up the reins, and the bronc
swung his head just enough to elude the grasp.
Unwilling to leave his new companion, the horse made
a small circle and came up on the brown's right.

Ben stayed quiet, let the chestnut relax and nuzzle
at the old gelding, then made his grab at the trailing
leather. The chestnut reared and pulled back hard,
but came forward against the strong curb. Ben kneed
the brown forward and began to backtrack the wide
trail the runaway had left. The wide-eyed chestnut
swung his head around and bared his teeth in an
attempt to tackle Ben's thigh, but a hard clout on the
nose stopped him. Ears flat, the horse settled into a
dragging trot alongside the steady brown.

The trailing was easy. Ben let the brown follow the
bent-over grass. Long before they reached the pool
and the cheerful spring, he could see a lone figure
trudging up the side of the rocky plateau. A short,
blocky man, unused to walking, teetering in his high
boots on the uncertain ground. Ben kept the two
horses to a walk, wondering just who had been riding
over his land. He shied away from his automatic use of
the word. No matter, someone was where they did not
belong.

Perce Tolliver heard the sound behind him, stopped
his laboring climb and waited, back to the oncoming
horses. The hoofbeats ceased just short of him, and
waited, forcing him to turn. On a sleek-headed brown
sat a familiar figure holding his chestnut snug by the
reins. A man he had visited in the guise of concern, a
man whose interference had put out the fire and lost

117

him another ranch. The man sat his horse just short of Tolliver and waited. No greeting, no nod of recognition, no questions. Just sat silent and out of reach.

Ben felt his anger rise and settle into distrust. Perce Tolliver wasn't what he expected. Ben could hear the wandering words of the old man as Harlow had sat over him in the darkened sickroom, talking on, speaking of greed and deceit, of the power and ruthlessness within Perce Tolliver. Now Ben found this same man riding his valley, close to his spring. Ben looked into the hard grey eyes of the rancher, and held his peace, waiting for the move.

Patience didn't suit Perce. And the shifting, restless chestnut was his.

"Damn it, man, give me the horse. Son of a bitch ain't broke, but he will be by the time we hit the home ranch."

Ben saw the anger build as the rancher spoke of the horse. He saw pure fury blaze the cool grey eyes.

"Your horse? Come get him."

With that Ben dropped the reins. The chestnut spooked at the abrupt move, then settled, unwilling to leave the brown.

"Get hold a him, mister. Or give me that brown. I ain't walking back from here."

"No reason for you to be up here. This land ain't yours, never will be. Belongs to me now. Serving notice to you. Keep off this range." Ben didn't know where the words came from, but he knew they were right. He was here to stay. He put a leg on the brown and started to move.

Tolliver jumped downhill, caught the circling horse by the bit shank, and hollered, "Mister, you'll swing for those words. You ain't nothing but a range bum with big ideas. You'll come down so fast no one will see you go."

The chestnut spooked at the commotion, got caught in the swinging quarters of the brown, and reared back as a hand jerked on his bit. Tolliver yanked again at the restive horse, then found the stirrup and swung up.

Head to head, knees almost touching in the close press of nervous horseflesh, the heavyset rancher and the pale-eyed rider watched each other. Their animals shifted precariously on the rough hillside, uneasy under their riders. Ben watched as building anger diffused a heavy flush across the older man's face. Tolliver glared at the younger man, hatred for the slight-built rider growing fast. This man had gotten in his way once too often.

The hard moment passed; the horses quieted, tempers cooled, and cold common sense brought Tolliver to jam his horse against the brown, staggering the animal slightly and moving it from his path. That was victory enough for now. Tolliver spurred the badly rattled chestnut back up the rock-hard trail beyond the plateau.

Ben watched the leaping horse carry its rider up and out of the small valley. He patted the sweaty brown neck and eased his hand on the reins. Now he understood the old man's obsession with Tolliver. The man drew blood when his true nature showed. The social visits to an invalid had been store dressing. Behind the expansive gestures and polite manner was the man his grandfather distrusted. On guard now, and having made his declaration, Ben turned back across the valley, staying to the narrowed trail and letting the broken path of the chestnut slowly struggle erect.

He headed back to the deep canyon, rode up the line along its lip. There was not sign of a suicide plunge of rotted bodies over the edge. And the further up the trail he went from the valley, the less the hard ground held prints. But there still were enough for him to read.

Ben off-mounted from the brown and squatted down to run his fingers lightly along a split shape. He didn't like what he read. Cattle wouldn't leave lush graze for the hardship of this trail on their own. Yet he could see no evidence of horses.

A heavy drop of water bounced off his cheek, followed by another, then a series of large clear drops wet his back. He looked up to the peak high above him. Beginnings of a dark storm were clear in the deepening sky. He wiped the beaded water from his face and checked his hand, surprised at the new mud covering his fingers.

He walked on, leading the reluctant brown into the wind. Then he stopped and sat on his heels, staring at the rain-spotted dust—at one blurred track, rounded, no defined edges, darkened by the rain. Not a split-hoofed print, but the broad and blunted track of a horse. Ben stood to look for a landmark, something to guide him back here after the storm.

What was coming would wipe out any more tracks he could find, so he continued up the trail, searching for another print to cement his suspicions. The search was slow, tedious, and futile. Only that one dust-covered print remained as proof of the riders who had to have pushed the herd up this far. He swung up on the brown and urged the old gelding forward. Headed into the storm was against his better judgment, and the old horse fought his rider, ran with his ears back, tail swishing in protest.

Finally Ben had to admit defeat. He could see nothing ahead but tangled brush and black sky. A smattering of sharp pellets swirled around him and the brown, a high wind gusted through the tall firs and brought waves of sleet, then stopped. The sun remained a tight yellow orb through a hole in the grey sky. Ben struggled with his slicker; the brown was restless beneath him and kept backing into the wind, fighting his rider.

Finally he released his tight hold on the reins, and the horse bucked into a run down the greasy trail. He would be back to seek out the trail of the cattle, but for now Ben shifted inside the slicker, trying to wrap it around himself tighter. The brown slogged over the high cut into the long valley, through the long empty grass and onto the winding path down to the dry warmth.

Chapter Eleven

Harlow Raynor had no compunction about making himself at home in this house. Hell, from the looks of things—the wadded blankets by the back door, the dust covering the big main room—the youngster hadn't settled in at all, had made no mark on the sprawling ranch house. The old man looked at the once-familiar walls with a detached bewilderment. He'd lived here a long time, he'd been gone only a few short months, yet he no longer dominated this place. It had the smell of a deserted house.

The rough main cabin, built when thick walls were a necessity, held no sense of his life here, of his daily existence for near to thirty-five years, of his wife dying here, of his daughter's day and night of birthing out the sullen-faced man who now had claim to the land.

There was some evidence of work getting done, just enough to give the old man hope: fence posts had been dug out and retamped; new rails were lashed to the sinking corral walls. But the hole in the barn roof was still there to threaten the walls. And there was only one horse in the pen, a miserable flea-bitten gray with a hammer head and scrub tail. Poor choice for a mount.

By the looks of it his boy was gone now, and gear with him. Just the runty gray remained, glad for the company, standing with nose touching the old black gelding tied to the rail. Be up to the springs. That's what he'd be doing. Checking out the life they gave this ranch.

The thought gave him hope. No man who knew cattle could look at that rich high graze and be unmoved by the desire to see his brand covering the land. The old man slumped into a heavy chair. This grandson of his was an odd one, tough to get a handle on. He wanted to dig at the boy, find the missing years. His two visits to the Stuart ranch, watching him struggle for air through burned lungs, seeing the pale eyes flash in recognition and turn away, had stuck a knife in him. The blade dug deep with the waste of those years.

Old age be damned. Harlow Raynor needed to get someone on to Perce. And soon. The chair accepted his tired body, and the old rancher let go in his mind with what he knew and suspected. The man wasn't going to lose again. Water. The old man's head nodded to his chest, then came up in a jerk. And then gave in to the ancient need to sleep. He dozed uneasily as the storm came down, shadows lengthened, and the rain pelted the empty ranch yard.

Seeing the strange black tied to the corral, hitched to an uncovered buggy, the horse shifting uncomfortably as it tried to maneuver downside from the wind. Ben quickly checked the sleet-covered yard, then said to hell with it and rode inside the barn. Anyone fool enough to plan an ambush wouldn't leave the horse tied as advertisement. He off-saddled fast, then shouldered his way out of the barn into the fierce wind and slipped the ice-shrouded black from the traces. The horse trotted sideways ahead of him to the shelter. Both horses deserved a good rubbing, but he wanted to find the driver of the black, so a quick bait of oats and a pile of hay would have to serve.

The house was dark; a legitimate visitor would have a lantern ready. Still uncertain inside the rambling structure, low and ominous in the storm-wild night, Ben went through the back door to the kitchen where he slept, and on to stand at the big room door. Loose and ready, he willed his eyes to accept the dark, to search out a movement that did not belong.

Everything was unfamiliar to him. Leaning against the doorjamb, he held still and waited, listened, searching for something.

"I'm here, boy. Waiting for you. Want to talk to you some."

The voice out of the darkness was the old man's: scratchy, thin, wavering. Ben Raynor shook his head. That old man had nothing he wanted to hear.

"Old man, I'll harness your horse; got a slicker and an old coat you can wear. Wet out there. And cold."

He turned from the doorway and picked up the wet jumper, shrugging it back on, taking time only to light a lantern and set it on the table. He wanted no more surprises. The old man's voice came at him again, but Ben focused his mind on the rustling of wet canvas, the flickering light, the obstinacy of the cold raingear.

The hair on the back of his neck bristled and stood

up. Ben turned slowly from the sheeting rain just outside the door and saw the old man. Framed by the dark passage, he was breathing hard, his face flushed and eyes too bright against the dim lantern light.

"Boy, you don't need to turn your back on me. I gave you this place. All I ask is that you listen."

Ben pitched his voice low, kept his words slow and deliberate: "You said it, old man. You gave me this place. I didn't want it. You gave it on your own. I owe you nothing beyond that."

The rash words he had spoken to Tolliver up on the high graze came back to him, instinctive words that accepted ownership of the ranch and its trouble. But he found it hard to look at the old man and soften his feeling for him. Years of bitterness stopped him from yielding to the simple request to listen.

Harlow Raynor shook his head slowly at the obstinacy of his grandson. There was no anger or passion in the flat denial, just a bitter refusal. A long look at the man standing at the back door, holding out a drying slicker, told him nothing. The blunt face had gotten back some color, the faded eyes no longer held the glaze of fever, but there still was no feeling to the tired face. This grandson of his was a walking dead man. He decided to gamble.

"Ain't nothing to you, is there, boy? Just waiting for the old man to leave so you can get on with your hiding in the darkness."

The words must have hit something. A whiteness thinned the mouth; a set came to the pale eyes. Then he settled, loosened his shoulders with visible effort, took another long breath and held out the slicker again, shaking it slightly as if to entice the old man.

Ben spoke as if he had not heard the probing words.

"It's time for you, old man. Time to go. You get no welcome from me. You threw that away years back."

Old man Raynor felt his frustration grow. He had to find the fire, and hate would do as well as a match.

"Sonny, you still fussing about your ma? I threw the hussy out. Carrying some man's woods colt, running around here like a filly just discovering a stud. We'd taught her better than that."

The slicker crackled as it dropped. A square hand jerked at the fragile arm, tore the old man away from his doorframe support, then pushed him to the center of the cold kitchen. This time he had gotten his response. The heavy gray head tumbled against the bird-thin chest, then snapped back upright as Ben shook the tormentor so close to him. Somewhere inside he knew what the old man was doing, knew the hateful words were a pointed tool, but the sharp edge brought back the years of shame and anger.

Everything tightened in Ben, twisting him to breaking as he held the old man off his feet. For a shocking moment the old man grinned, glad to see the fire in those dead eyes. Then, as he hung suspended, feet just grazing the hard floor, heavy coat bunched at his chin, he stared into the eyes so much like his. Close to the raging man, so close he could see the veins pounding across his forehead, pulsing at his temple, old man Raynor watched a tightly disciplined control pull back the fury.

The square hand softened its grip at his throat, the floor becoming solid once again beneath his feet. His breath came in gasps; phlegm choked him in a spitting cough. An arm held him, a hand touched his shoulder and guided him back to the long front room, settled him in the heavy chair near the cold fireplace.

Harlow Raynor smiled at his success, grinned at the harsh face profiled in the wavering light from the kitchen lantern.

"Boy—" He held silent for a long moment. "Ben. It's time we stopped this fighting each other and took to talk. We're all that's left, and I ain't got a whole lot more. Want to know about you, boy, and what happened to your ma. I need to know, even if you think I ain't got the right."

He watched the square face that had turned slightly toward him at the bargaining words. Then he continued his appeal.

"I need to know what happened to you, son, why you don't care. It's a pure pity how you feel."

Then Ben Raynor knew with a gut-aching certainty that shamed him: these next few minutes could give him something again or forever shut him off from people, to live isolated and alone. The two years past had eaten him day by day, leaving behind a dry shadow that walked and talked, a thin casing around an empty soulless being. This was his second chance. But the words that would shed the years were hard in coming, the feelings painful, and buried deep.

A thin hand touched him, pushed against his shoulder gently.

"Light a fire, boy, and talk. Tell me. And I'll tell you. 'Cause there is more here than just me and you. Others out there is heading into trouble. And you can do something, if'n you can learn to care."

The square hands that laid the fire, that picked out long dry splinters to burn hot and fast, shook ever so slightly. Ben struck the match to bring the logs to life, to warm the old man hunched in the big chair, sending licks of yellow light throughout the room. His instincts flinched at the strike of fire, the hot touch near his fingers, but he settled back on his haunches and carefully watched the growing flames. The next moments were up to him.

"Two years ago I had a ranch, a wife, two sons. A good ranch, running a bunch of cattle on a fine piece of graze. My graze. Been there seven, eight years. Your daughter—my mother—came to live with us three years before. Left a husband behind somewhere she didn't want to talk about. We were glad to have her."

A silence came before he spoke again, a short silence that that let the ghost of the woman who bonded the two men live again in the walls where she had once lived. Then Ben continued.

"A cattle company bought into the valley. Wanted all the land, not just what was open. Had lots of money, a tough foreman paying out a gunman's wage. They brought in a lot of trouble." His voice wore thin, almost unintelligible, then he picked up again, the words coming fast.

"They wanted our piece. We had a good stream running our land, stayed running all summer. I wouldn't sell. It was where I belonged, a good place for our kids to grow up. Then threats started. Hard times in town, cattle run till they dropped, horses scattered, stolen. Even the townsfolk wanted us to sell, wanted the trade the big company would bring. But we chose to stay."

The old man coughed, phlegm again thick in his

throat. An answering flare in his belly warned him, but he spat into the fire and watched his grandson, waited for the words he knew were coming.

"The bosses came one day, said it was their last offer, our last chance. Offered a good price, enough to move us somewhere and start again. But we chose to stay. I drove them off with a rifle. Sent one man home with a busted arm. And they came back. That night they came back. . . ."

His voice dropped again. The next words were slow in coming.

"They came back. With guns and fire. Burned us out, about two in the morning. Must have circled the house with kerosene and lit it in several places. I was in the barn, up with a breech-birth cow. I smelled smoke and came out yelling. It took only one shot to bring me down."

He rubbed his hand through the copper hair, twisting the gray line streaked in the curls.

"They let me crawl up to the house. Left me to lie there and listen to my family scream and die inside. My legs wouldn't hold me. I couldn't stand, just crawl some. I lay there and listened to them burn."

The two men sat in the dark silence. The old man put out a hand to reach for the tight shoulder of his grandson. Habit moved the younger man away, and the roughened hand found only the shell of the steaming jacket and then nothing. Abruptly Ben's voice continued with the damning tale.

"Townspeople were there. Seemed like the whole damned town. They watched the fire. The company men held them, so these neighbors, folks I'd known for years, sat on their horses and watched us burn.

They left me on the ground, figured I'd be dead soon.

"But I didn't die. A long time later I pulled myself up, found the gray horse, who'd come down for hay. I dug into the ruins, found the lumps that had been my wife and child. Found my mother holding one son. I buried them. Rode away and left it. Never went back."

The damning voice hesitated for just a moment, then repeated itself: "I killed them for a ranch and my pride. I killed them. Then I rode away, and never went back."

Chapter Twelve

Harlow Raynor wanted desperately to speak, to say anything that would take away the knife edge of what he had just heard. But he held his words. This was a hell that Ben Raynor had to live through on his own.

The small fire in the stone fireplace sputtered and died down. Hot coals left enough light that the tired old man could see his grandson, could count the deep, etched lines at his eyes and mouth. Face turned to the fire, eyes blank, it looked as if nothing had been changed by the tearing words.

Then a rough choking sound came from the hunched body; awful sounds that broke, then steadied. Then Ben Raynor tried again.

"It's your turn, grandpap. You owe me, I'm listening."

Harlow Raynor faced the same struggle, found the needed words hard in coming.

"Ben, your ma never would tell me her man's name, or where he went. Just said she loved him and it was a mistake, one she would never regret. I didn't throw her out. Her ma did. Couldn't stand the shame here in town. Netta died the next year. I took the blame to ease her, but she couldn't live with what she'd done."

Ben knelt down to throw in a log, poke a stick and

stir up a thin blaze. He knew there was more to come. The old man, silent beside him, coughed again several times, and settled back in his chair.

"It's this ranch—all that's left of us Raynors. I know you now, see why a ranch is something you don't want. And this war ain't nothing of your doing. But I know Perce Tolliver. He be a wild one who never tamed down. He wants this ranch, that spring. All them springs."

Ben found he could hear the words, understand their importance, and not flinch from the raw memories they drew up. The choice was up to him now.

"What makes you so sure, where no one else here sees anything?"

Harlow Raynor grinned; he liked this question, meant the boy had made his choice. A heavy cough took him, shaking his thin body, almost doubling him in the huge chair. A hand gently held his shoulder, offered its support as the spasm continued. He tried to speak, but that damned phlegm thickened his words. Another good spit into the fire raised a hiss of steam, then he could speak more easily.

"Knew the man years ago. Came down with me and Bob Mosser, Ellis Landry, when we brought a herd in from Montana. Wanted to see the world. A real hell-raiser. Fired him once we settled here. Took off with one of my best roping horses.

"Didn't think much of him then, a runty kid with carrot-red hair and a wicked eye. Kept running into his name over the years, never nothing good. Not real bad, just rough. Got freezed out, lost a wife, started over again. Heard some time later he'd lost again, and that another woman walked out on him. And now he's here, riding all over and buying up graze.

"That one don't plan to freeze or burn again. Don't care 'bout the other fellow, just ain't going to take no more hard luck. He rode up here past fall. Came right in and walked all through my home with never a yes or no. Then found me in town, told me of his look-see, how he was fixing to take over around here. Figured he could wait till I died."

Breathing came harder to the old man, forcing him to stop, to sit back and wait. Ben built up the fire again, watching the old man shiver in the greatcoat, unable to find warmth. Then he sat back on his haunches, willing to wait for the rest.

"Told me all this with a light in his eye and a tongue as smooth as honey. Made it all sound nice and neighborly, but making sure to let me know the words were lying. The bastard.

"I'm betting the fire was his. He must of thought it would drive the sisters to him. But you messed that one. He was expecting to pick up this place from no one after I was gone. Real cheap. But you got into that, you got in his way again. It's turning out your fight, even if you don't want it. Seems to have put its own name on you."

The tired voice wore down. The old man sat deep in the familiar chair with closed eyes. God. This thing eating him was a terror. Be good to hand on the fight. He looked over at his grandson from under half-opened lids; the grim set to the face had eased, the pale eyes now reflected only firelight, no longer holding a lingering pain. This one would be all right. He finished his thought out loud.

"It's your fight now, boy. Up to you."

Ben spoke as if more words had passed between them. Words asking and answering about what would be done.

"Rode up to the springs today. The Stuart women are missing over two hundred head. Wanted to stay and sort out the trail, but this damn storm beat me to it. There'll be nothing left tomorrow but a short herd and a muddy trail. When this storm is over I'm going to back up, follow the herd best I can. I owe the sisters that much. It's a start."

Ben looked at his grandfather; the heavy white head nodded slightly, as if in agreement, then another cough shook the frail body. The old man needed hot food and a warm bed. Ben rose and went to the semidark kitchen, the flickering kerosene lamp just enough to let him see.

A bit of scrounging through his meager supplies dug out two airtights of beans, and a wet trip to the shed out back produced a venison steak cut from a hanging carcass. . . . A meal for the two men was soon ready.

Ben stood near the big chair and looked down at the sunken head resting on the bony chest. He did not need to touch the old man to know. The cranky, contentious, hard-headed pioneer was dead.

The body was light, like a child's. Ben carried it to a room behind the kitchen, a room shut off and made up as if waiting for this man's final return. He placed the thin body down gently and pulled the blanket up over the white hair. He closed the door and walked in silence back to a solitary meal and a bed of blankets rolled out near the back door.

Bright sun cleared the valley, teasing with its last memory of summer heat. A bite of winter wind came with the clearing air. Ben harnessed the black and set his rig on the brown. Today he had to clean up, settle the old man's death, talk to Nora Stuart. Then he was back up to the mountains.

He felt no sorrow for the old man. Mourning would come in its own way, in its own time. Pain had cleared him, and he was free. The thin body weighed even less this morning; wrapped in the old green-striped blanket he laid it in a bed of straw in the livery wagon, and drove the black at a good trot into the town of Gladstone. The brown gelding, tied to the back of the wagon, protested every step.

The big doctor looked up from his breakfast coffee at the sound of brisk steps coming to his door, and was pleased to see his first patient of the day. Usually early visitors were emergencies, but not this one. This was a success, a patient healing nicely. The doctor's homely face broke into a smile, then folded back to its customary sternness as he listened.

So. The old man had died in the night. And died at his own ranch. That was more fitting than dying here in town. He did not bother to question the grandson, just nodded his understanding.

"All right. Bring him in to the back room. I will take care of him, write out the death certificate. We will bury him with Netta. That is what he wanted. The town can say good-bye today, we will have the service tomorrow. He may not have been easy to live with, or to love, but he was a good man, the first man here. And this town respected the man, even if you do

137

not."

The words were meant to dig. Ben let the comment go; there wasn't time to explain, nor the need to. He only dropped his head in acceptance, then watched the big man, who moved very slowly to stand.

"Take care of him," Ben said. "I've made my peace, now there is something to finish."

Ben set his hat back on and walked from the office. The particulars of the next few days were important. He needed supplies, a warm coat, a visit to the Stuart ranch, and then he could get back to that one blurred hoofprint.

He stood for a moment on the walkway, watching the activity on the street. He had seen something that the doctor, just inside by his window, could not see. He shifted his weight, restless now, and alert. Then he stepped from the walkway into the new mud and angled across the street to a horseman tying up at the marshal's office.

Dr. Halderson watched his ex-patient step into the street. He took note of the new life to the man, the quickened strides as he moved through the early traffic. Something was different. There was a willingness to meet his eye, a clear set to the man, that was new. The doctor watched Raynor meet up with another man at the base of the steps. It was Perce Tolliver. Early for him to be in town, too.

Town Marshal Cable Orton also watched the old man's grandson cross through the mud, saw him meet up with Tolliver just outside this office. He eased himself up from the chair, tin cup loosely held in his hand. This meet-up could be interesting. He refilled the cup and went to the office door. He opened the door and leaned against the frame, eyeing the two men standing apart as if squaring off for a fight. Could be very interesting. He took an impatient sip of coffee, and burned his lips with its heat.

Ben met the rancher's hard gray eyes with a level gaze. Tolliver returned the stare, recognizing his opponent, then tipped his head as if in acknowledgment of the impending fight. Ben saw beyond Tolliver to the big man looming over them in the open doorway. He did not take his gaze from the blocky man, but spoke over his head.

"The old man died last night, out to his ranch. I brought him in, to the doc's. Funeral tomorrow."

Even though he had known of the inevitability of this death, Cable Orton felt a stab of pain. The old man had been this country, here before the town, before any of the others. His death took an innocence from the basin, left everything wide open.

Orton glanced at the short, stocky rancher who stood there listening. Triumph glinted in the gray eyes, at odds with the words of condolence directed at the younger man, words that carried a warning to the alert marshal.

"That's too bad, boy. I'm real sorry the old man's gone. Now there ain't no one left to head up this basin. A real shame," said Tolliver.

His own anger caught Ben off balance. Outraged anger that this man, standing so casually on the splintered steps, would make an old man's death an instant victory. He fought the impulse to answer Tolliver's goad, to tell him of the old man's suspicions.

139

He knew for certain now what this rider had been doing up in the high spring graze: checking over what soon would be his graze.

He choked on the hot words, struggled to keep the fury from his face. He didn't want this man knowing there was someone after him. His vision cleared, his balance set, Ben stepped around the still-smiling rancher to come closer to the big lawman.

"The doc said to tell you he'll send a report later." Ben let the remnants of anger settle. "I'll head out now, be back when I'm done, if you got questions. Will be at the R Cross permanent."

He wanted the rancher to hear those words, to know them for acceptance of the fight. Tolliver responded to form, eyes flashing, shoulders stiffening as if insulted. Then he smiled at his new neighbor.

Orton watched the younger man as he spoke. So he's decided to stay, he thought. Must have come to terms with the old man. He saw a flash of clear light in the pale blue eyes, an eagerness to the wiry body. He looked past Ben to the older rancher, then came back to Ben. Weighing, searching, judging. Ben stood there and waited under the scrutiny.

Tolliver broke the line building between the marshal and the ex-drifter.

"Just came to tell you, Marshal, that I'm planning on having a big shindig out to my ranch. Some time the end of the month. Kind of a celebration. We can make part of it a wake for the old man. Want to invite you special. I may be needing a real steady hand come early morning, kind of a police force, to get folks home."

He took the last three steps of the stairs past Ben

and up beyond the marshal, then turned as if the thought had just come to him.

"That invite is for you too, Raynor—now that you're a big rancher in these parts. Be looking up to talking with you. We got some business to discuss."

The dig brought high color to Ben's face. He turned his back to the blocky rancher. Tolliver watched him walk away, amused and pleased that his shot had gone home. He spoke to the lawman, shaking his head in manufactured dismay, the faded red strands flopping over his baldness.

"Damndest thing. I offer a kind word and that one walks away. Not the old man his grandpappy was. A no-count drifter. Too bad."

Perce tipped his head to the frowning marshal and continued his way down the echoing wooden walk. Today was his day to invite the town, and be damned to the death of one old man.

His few purchases completed at Hiller's, Ben mounted the brown and headed out toward the Stuart place. The exchange with Tolliver burned deeply into him. He had given in to the flush of anger, and the other man had the victory. It was a declaration of war, a hidden war with the intent to drive him from the basin, or bury him under it. Tolliver had made it plain, and Ben's anger would make it easy.

Intent on the events of the past hour, Ben paid no attention to his horse. The brown picked up an easy gallop and turned by instinct onto the narrow track that would take him home. His strides lengthened, and it was only when the small ranch yard came into sight that Ben abruptly slowed the horse, sending a shower of mud up from the soggy ground. The brown bounced to a hard stop, then whickered nervously.

Nora Stuart stepped to the horse's head, wiping at the smattering of mud on her sleeve. She had recognized the familiar bald face and was anxious to see his rider. She snugged the brown up by the cheekpiece of his bridle, and stared up at Ben.

A smile lightened her face. Something was different in the man on the restive brown. The distance in the blunt face was replaced by a soft and easy smile. He sat the horse with a loose grace, slouched in the battered saddle. Nora anticipated the words, wondering to herself. And was surprised at what he said.

Ben removed his hat. "Ma'am, the old man died last night. Went real easy, out to his ranch. Doc says burial's tomorrow. But that ain't why I'm here. Got some business to talk with you."

He looked down at the woman standing so close to his leg. Her face was framed with the bright sun, its light softening the pull of her hair, the weathered roughness to her face, and added a glint to her eyes. A woman to come home to, to work alongside her man. He caught up his thoughts and went back to the business—business that would unbalance her, take the gentle smile from her mouth. His voice came too harshly to mask his distress.

"Was up to your springs. You're short over two hundred head. Found a trail headed up beyond the peak. Left only a few marks that I could read, and the storm took those. Going back up there now. Figure you would know the trails over the pass, what was beyond them. I plan to track down your herd and get

142

them back."

It was a long speech for Ben, and the news was painful. He saw the dismay cover her face, then saw the fight to regain her composure, saw her jaw set, her hand push at the bony head of the itchy brown. She spoke without thinking.

"Don't you go. I'll ask Mr. Tolliver. You still aren't strong enough, and I know Perce will take care of this."

She couldn't have said anything more wrong. Knowing it was a mistake, but in his wildness not caring, Ben found the image of the smug-faced rancher heating his words, damning Nora's concern.

"Lady, it's a good bet that Tolliver's behind the theft. The old man knew. Tolliver wants those springs—yours *and* mine—anyway he can get them. And robbing you blind is just the beginning."

Fury brought a deep red to Nora's face. That this man would accuse another of theft without proof, that he would deny the acts of kindness during his illness, that he would smear a good man's name without conscience. . . . Her anger grew.

She opened her mouth, words sputtering to be said. Ben put the brown gelding in a spin. He recognized the sickness in his gut; his ill-timed words had driven away the woman he wanted to bring close. He could not stay and see out the anger he had called up. He put spurs to the brown and the horse kicked out indignantly. Ben would find the cattle, face Tolliver with the guilt, and . . . His thoughts went no further.

Chapter Thirteen

This was the last look around. The gray beneath him shifted restlessly, tail twitching, eager to run. It felt strange to be saddled up and moving out. For the past two years he had done nothing but run; this time he felt a loss as he rode from the R Cross. Given a chance he would be back to settle down here.

The climb up to the springs was fast. The gray tackled the rocks and winding path with an eagerness lacking in the older brown. Ben gave the little horse his head, pausing only to catch his breath at the flat rock near the top before bursting down into the lush valley. At the Stuart spring, the remaining cattle picked up their heads in vague curiosity as horse and rider galloped through their home.

The trail was washed clear alongside the canyon rim. Ben reined in the gray at a familiar tree-split rock. Right here he had seen that one blurred and softened track. Behind him the canyon twisted and widened to rise up and form part of the backside of the valley. The trail paralleled the lip for a short distance, then wound into steep forest of fir swelling toward the peak, thinning into a rugged trail that no grazing animal would willingly travel.

He shrugged into the heavy blanket coat, and silently thanked the owner of the Emporium for taking his marker. He owed a debt in the small town now. He had to come back. The trail climbed high, a snaking path through tumbled rock and soaring fir. The gray clambered past the trees, then snorted in surprise as they came out to a high meadow. Ben reined in the gray and allowed him to shift backside to the cold wind.

Driving cattle this far was a chore no one would take on pure gamble. Whoever had stolen the cattle had had a set buyer and plenty of help. Ben touched the gray and easily followed the faint markings of a trail across the high grass. The line was punctuated by water-flattened droppings from two hundred head.

They went back into a stand of towering spruce, interspersed with smaller fir. Finally he rode out of the now-stunted stand of trees to a boulder-covered pass. The leavings from the cattle were still visible across the wasteland. Behind him was the high meadow he had crossed, below that the dark line of high fir. Ahead was the continuous flow of peaks and shallow dips that led slowly downhill to the backside of the mountain range.

Ben shivered against the high buttoned collar of the thick coat. The cold had not yet turned to snow, but the ground was icy hard and slippery from the remnants of sleet. He shivered again and slapped the gray neck. The sound echoed long in the thin air. He touched the horse, and the mustang picked his way with care across the lichen-covered rocks and sparse grass.

Darkness came too quickly, sending the gray tripping and stumbling on unseen rocks. Finding a small meadow, Ben off-saddled and hobbled the gray. A fire came up fast, and he cooked thin strips of the venison haunch. Hot coffee and beans with the meat filled him for now. The gray cropped viciously at the browned vegetation, yet did not stray far from the fire, seeming to want its protection.

Ben rolled in his blankets and lay cold for a long time. Sleep could not come through his tiredness. In the dark images came rolling over him: hard pictures of burning barns, cattle disappearing in midair, an old man slumped invisible in a chair. But most of all there were a woman's deep warm eyes, shaded by worry, then turning away from him in anger.

The gray stamped his feet against the cold. A distant howl came faintly to Ben. Another howl joined the first, then a ring of voices from an unseen valley below. Ben strained to listen, intent on the sounds. Then he slept.

The cold dawn brought him awake. A few dulled coals remained of his fire. They came back to life with added bits of dried grass and wood. Reheated coffee and hard biscuits made enough breakfast. The gray needed water; Ben mounted the horse and sent him deeper down into the trees, searching for a stream.

He had lost the trail two days back. It was guesswork now that kept him riding, wandering aimlessly, following shadows. Down from the high fir, he had ridden into an unexpected stand of lodgepole pine, and had circled back on himself before hitting the far side.

His face itched from beard stubble, and his meager supplies were almost gone. At a twist in the steep trail he was on, an hour or two back, he had glimpsed a small cabin far down below. The path vaguely headed in its direction. He spurred the tired gray into a trot over the worn path. There might be someone ahead who could answer questions.

The cabin was visible from between the high-standing fir. Ben slowed the gray to a walk across the clearing right up to the simple log house. He called his hello, and got no answer. Water sparkled in a rough-built trough near a lean-to. A sway-backed paint mare stood in the small pen adjoining, head lifted in interest as she scented out the gray.

The mustang buried his muzzle in the ice-cold water up to his eyes, reveling in the good abundance, and Ben eased his feet from the stirrups, letting the stiffness drain from his legs. Nobody was home from the looks of things, but gear was hung carefully on the lean-to walls, and there were remnants of a small summer garden. All these things spoke of someone living here, and planning to stay.

Wouldn't be the rustlers. Too much pride in the small cabin. But whoever lived here might have seen the herd come down the mountainside; might know where it would be headed. Turning in the saddle, Ben could see the faint lines of the trail he had been following outlined in the chipped gray rock and thinned-down trees from the pass. Whoever lived in this cabin might well have something for him.

"Don't move a muscle, mister. Set right there on your horse."

The voice was thin, high, female. And hard. Knowing exactly what it wanted. Ben froze.

"Set easy. Now, turn around. Face me and let's get this over. Slow, mind you, and mighty careful."

The gray turned in a small circle. Ben sat quietly, his feet still dangling free. He found a young woman standing on the cabin steps, a girl almost. She was thin and small, but the shotgun she held was cradled in her hands like a friend, a companion of long standing. Bright blue eyes looked hard into Ben's pale ones. The girl shook her head slightly, blew hard and short like a spooked bronc.

"Hell, you ain't one a them. But that don't get you clean with me. Be a start, though."

Ben kept his silence. "Them" could be his men. The quiet grew. He found the blue eyes going over him with a hard and demanding look that made him aware of his short beard, the smell coming from his week-long clothes. She must have caught the chagrin on his face, for she broke into a smile.

"Sure ain't pretty, is you, mister? Kinda puny looking, and my old mare can smell you even though she be upwind."

Then she laughed, and Ben realized she was not a child, but a full-grown woman, as she leaned sideways to put the butt of the shotgun down beside her, one hand still holding the barrel. Her dress pulled tight across her breasts, swinging free under the wash-worn fabric. She followed his gaze and her laughter ceased, to be replaced by a wildness in her eyes, a fullness to her mouth.

"What you looking at, mister? There ain't nothing here for you."

The young woman twisted a hand through thick blond hair falling loose and tangled down her back. Each breath brought her breasts rising high, brought Ben more awareness of the woman who stood before him. She lowered her eyes, looked up sideways at the pale rider before her. Ben nodded once and tipped his hat, then made a motion to ride on.

Hattie Childress knew now what she had been told. Her ma had come a few years past, to stay for a time and die. Her death had slowly killed the man who had been Hattie's father—a rough man, who had lived out his life stunned from the War Between the States. Unable to speak of love, he had let Hattie's mother go, had raised up the child in the safe high mountains, and had waited patiently for Hattie's mother to return.

She remembered her mother's words: "Daughter, stay away from most men. They ain't worth spit. But sometime you will see a man and your belly will light with fire. You'll feel heavy inside, slow, as if each touch would burn you. That's a man you can love. It won't last long, but the feeling ain't to be forgot. It's what we is made for. Your father did that to me. Can't stand to live with him, to look at him for long. But he touch me and that feeling just make me sink to my knees and wait for him. Girl, it's what there be in living."

Hattie had waited the years. Men had ridden past her doorway, and she had shown them the shotgun, sending them on in the dark with scorn.

Until this man. His pale blue eyes, the wild-streaked copper hair. His strong face too white beneath a new burn, the square hands tipped with strong fingers. She could feel those hands on her body, feel that mouth take hers, feel those pale eyes own her body. She broke into a run after the speckled gray horse, dragging the shotgun with her.

Ben stopped the little horse. The shock of his response to this woman, still a child only, unnerved him. Two years had gone since he had wanted a woman. He'd been in a couple of fancy houses drunk with the boys, wild with anger, demanding service. But he had been unable to perform. Like a barbwire-cut stud, there had been only the memories.

But this woman had caught him short, brought all the wild surges back. Her voice cut him, turned him in the saddle.

"Mister, you want something. Something I can give you."

No question, just a statement. He fought himself, and lost. Then spoke. He did need something from her. But not what he wanted.

"Looking for some men driving a herd of two hundred or so cattle. 'Bout three, four weeks back, maybe more. I want them."

Hattie shied at the words. This wasn't what she wanted. A hand shielded her face as she looked up at the sharp-etched face. Pale eyes burned into hers, but the voice broke off the contact, the unwanted and ordinary words continued.

"Probably three or four men. I need to know if they went through here, the brand the horses wore, where they might be headed. You live up here, you see everything. I need your help."

Ben choked on his thoughts, coughed through a thickened throat, shook his head in bewilderment at

151

the tingling in his body.

Hattie reached up and placed her small, hard-calloused hand along Ben's thigh. They both looked down at the tanned fingers resting lightly against the muscled leg. Ben felt a burn where the tips touched so softly. Hattie's clear voice came to him again, tearing his thoughts away from the slender, delicate, all-consuming hand that lay on his leg.

"They tried to stop here. Four men and a tired herd a cows. I let them water, but they wanted more. A big blond-headed ranny thinking he only needed to smile and I'd take him in. An ugly skinny old man, ganted up hard. Talked like I wasn't here. They was headed down through Wild Canyon to some ranch near the border. Got them a place for them cattle there."

That was all he needed. Four men and a tired herd. A name, a description, and a direction. There was nothing more. Ben thought to gig the gray, then reined him in so sharply the gelding reared and squealed his protest.

Hattie Childress stood alone in the hard, frozen yard, the big shotgun, still muzzle up, resting over her arm. It was crazy. Ben kneed the gray over to the small woman, leaned down, and lifted her head with his left hand. Standing on tiptoe, her full mouth reached for his and held to it, drawing him into her body, offering him everything he could want.

The gray shifted against the falling weight of his rider and broke the kiss. Ben looked into the smoky blue eyes of the woman, at the shiny mouth bruised and wounded.

Feeling lost, a fool, he only closed his eyes and turned the gray to ride out, not looking behind him to see the lush mouth tighten to a thin line, the hot eyes turn to blue ice. The tired gray responded sluggishly to his spurs and headed down into the badlands, leaving Hattie Childress alone.

Chapter Fourteen

Perce heard the horse before he could see its rider. He stepped back into the house and put his hand on a rifle, brought it outside to lean it up against the wall. This country was settled now, but it didn't hurt to be on guard. Old habits died hard.

The laugh was on him. He watched Nora Stuart dismount from the fine blue dun gelding and wrap the reins around the railing. At the bottom of the steps she paused and looked up at him.

"Mr. Tolliver, good morning. I got word you had some things you wanted talked over with my sister and me. Emily will be along soon."

She came up the steps then, and smiled over her shoulder at the rancher who finally remembered his manners and held the heavy door open for her. The faded gray eyes smiled back, and Nora walked into the old Jackman house. Inside it was evident that Tolliver had already left his mark: heavy furniture, old and multi-scarred, woven Indian rugs on the walls, gear thrown in corners, and a bottle with a glass on the large desk. There was no sign left of Ceily Jackman and her twenty years of spinsterhood.

Tolliver spoke first. "Mrs. Stuart, ah, Nora. I need your kind help. Yours, and your sister's. I've gone

155

and invited the whole valley here, and then realized that I need a woman to get everything going. Ain't put on a shindig since my wife was gone. Forgot all the things need doing. Would the two of you be so kind as to help? Wanted to get you over here to see the place, get some ideas, point me in the right direction."

Nora felt a sigh of relief. This was simple. "Why, Mr. Tolliver, of course." This would be a way to return all his favors, his generosities. Nora found herself studying the man, watching him with Ben's accusation in her mind. But this kindly and helpful man could not be the one responsible for her loss.

Perce saw the smile and read it clearly: Pleased to be able to help the poor, misguided bachelor man. Pleased to be given a chance to pay all his kindness back. The Stuart women were deeper in his debt. His quickened senses caught another sound; he strode across the wide plank floor and pulled back the door just as the other sister topped the last step. An expansive arm sweep invited her inside to sit next to Nora and discuss the details.

Nora read over the list while Emily chattered with Tolliver. There would be a lot to do between now and the party, and she had to find time still to bring down the remaining cattle and move the stallion and mares back up to the high valley. The thoughts reminded her of her talk with Ben, and of the anger he'd revealed. She spoke her mind, then immediately felt a loss.

"Mr. Tolliver, last week Ben Raynor came by with bad news. I wanted your help, but felt we had asked enough of you already. But it is something I cannot tackle alone. Orton's authority is limited to town, but he has sent out word."

Now that she had started, Nora became uncomfortable. Tolliver sat impassively in his big chair, and she felt as if she had blundered into something. She felt Ben's heated words deep within her.

Tolliver straightened a little as he watched the woman. He knew what was coming, had heard the word through town. He had been waiting for the little lady to come to him.

"Ben rode up to the spring, said that two hundred cattle were missing. He was headed back to the mountains to track as far as he could, hopefully find the herd. We haven't heard from him since."

She rested for a moment, wiped a hand tiredly across her face, and missed the anger pushing at Tolliver's smiling face. She had gone this far, and concern for Ben rode her strong.

"Could you send someone up after him? I've got to know what is happening. Together, perhaps, the cattle will be found."

Her words were a convenience for Perce; the favor she asked was a good cover. Sending someone after Raynor was just what Perce planned on doing. Only not to nicely bring him back, or help him find the herd, but to bury him up in the hills and bring back the proof of his guilt. Lay it all on Ben Raynor, dead and left back in the mountains.

Perce rose wearily to his feet, concern for these two women strong on his weathered face.

"I'll get Windy Dawes and a couple of good hands and send them after Raynor for you. We'll make certain everything is settled up in the hills, and try to find your cattle for you. Don't you worry."

157

There was a small settlement ahead. A hard-scuffed rancher some miles ago had growled a few words at Ben. No, he hadn't seen a herd, no, no one came up this way from the mountain. Yeah, he could ask in town, pick up some supplies. Ben rode on.

He'd wandered in the wasteland long enough and was no closer to the herd. Only the woman three days behind him had given him anything to use. A description, a direction. And a kiss that came back to him every night, racking his sleep with wild dreams that shook him awake.

Face drawn fine, shoulders slumped against the continued weariness, Ben tied the gray to a sagging rail in front of a yellow painted building, peeling now, and badly faded. A sign had once said that drinks were offered inside the Nugget Saloon, but the letters had bleached to a memory, and only the darkened outline of one word, drinks, remained to call the passerby.

Ben faced three steps up the wooden building; he sighed deeply and took each one slowly. The inside of the bar offered no more than what was visible outside: a long plank on three barrels, the remains of a framed mirror holding only dustwebs ran across the back of the room. One man stood behind the plank, two others were drinking and talking in low tones at the only table in the cold room.

A drink wasn't what he wanted, but the single light of the saloon was the only sign of human occupation in the small settlement. Ben ordered a beer; the barkeep grinned and shoved a shot of whiskey across to him.

"Out of beer. Be out of whiskey soon, then we close up." Bare facts of the end of a town. Ben was curious through his tiredness.

"What happened? You just going to fold up and drift away?" The man behind the bar only shook his head. There was nothing much to tell.

"Ain't really a town here, just a stopping place. Used to be hunters up in these mountains, a few miners, one or two small ranches. Nothing left now but Isherton's and he trades down to the territory. We all going to dry up and blow down the valley. What you want here, mister? On the run, are you?"

The question was beyond range courtesy, but the slow smile and lack of real interest kept the barkeep safe from retribution. He didn't care about the answer, and it showed.

Tired, too tired to be cagey, to ease into his questions, Ben questioned the bored man:

"Looking for a herd of cattle, passed through somewhere around here about three weeks ago. Had four men driving them, one old ranny called Windy, a big blond-haired gent, and two drunks. Know anything about them?"

To the bartender, the slight, pale-eyed man was a puzzle. Nothing about him said law, or stock detective, yet there was something that kept him from being on the other side. Whatever the man was, the answer to his question was easy, and he was free to give it. The whiskey would be gone soon, and then so would he.

"Yep. Them you described came here. The drunks sucked up the last of the beer and took most of the rest of my whiskey. Paid for it, though. Rode outta

159

here with heads feeling like burst melons. Fought it out with one too many bottles afore they left. The old skinny one was cussing them and cursing their ma and pa. Yep, 'bout that time ago. Said they was headed to Isherton's Wide Z, had a home for the beeves there."

It had taken Ben another drink and a few coins before the barkeep let him go. He had with him vague directions to the Wide Z. After some searching he finally crested a bluff that looked down over a wide-spreading ranch set at the wide end of a flat river valley. He reined in the gray and sat for a short time, pondering his next move.

The spread was out of the way, off the main line for a grub-line rider; the men down there would be suspicious of any rider, guarded in their acceptance of what he said, controlled by the presence of two hundred stolen cattle with fresh-worked brands.

He settled on a run from the law, on looking for a place to hole up for the winter. Chances were good those same suspicious men would accept such a man, and his week's growth of beard and dirt-crusted clothes would aid his story.

He angled the gray down the sloping trail. By the time he had ridden near enough to see the colors on the horses milling in the pen, a sizeable group of men stood in casual watch. As he approached, one detached himself from the group, and came out to stand in his way, left hand firm on one pistol at his thigh, the other hand up to stop him.

Ben stared into dark brown eyes, watched them read him over and judge him in a quick moment. The man had an arrogant stand, long head tilted sideways, heavy mustache drooping on each side of a small, thin-lipped mouth. The dark eyes held no humor, and flickered only briefly as the man spoke his piece.

"You. Out. Off this ranch. We want no riders here what don't belong."

At his caustic words the remaining men formed a thick line behind their spokesman, hands resting easy within reach of weapons, shoulders shifting restlessly in the absence of action. One man, tall, broad backed, blond hair catching the thin fall sun, came close to the boss, almost touching the older man's back. He spoke words in a low voice, and the tall man angled his head to listen. He glanced up at Ben, then brought his head around to look at the talker.

It was the grin that Ben remembered; and in one easy motion he swung the gray around and lifted him into a full gallop. He could hear shouting behind him, then one high voice came clear:

"Goddammit, get the horses. Don't let Raynor get away. Morse, get my dun and that bay."

It was Blake Morse, the arrogant cowhand at the Stuart ranch that Nora had sent packing. Who had gone to work for Tolliver. Whatever reason had brought him here, Ben knew it was the connection between Tolliver and the Wide Z.

He dug spurs to the tired gray, demanding more speed. The wiry mustang gave his heart and tore up the ragged side of the bluff and out onto the flat mesa beyond. Once off the flat and into the trees he would have a chance. There were a number of blind canyons and zigzagged trails that would hide him. It was his only chance.

The mustang bellied down and ran, the head start

Ben's unexpected exit had given them an edge. Fresh horses were to the pursuers' advantage, but they lost precious time to catch and saddle. Once off the mesa, the gray was tireless in dodging between trees and twisting through matted brush. Ben drove the horse hard, headed toward a small canyon where he had seen a barren trail.

Off the gray's back, he led the animal up a narrow track. Partway up he ground-tied the heaving horse and slipped back down to wipe out the tracks. The gray stayed head down, grateful for the break. Ben led the horse the last few steps and remounted at the top. There were still miles to travel before dark. He took a moment to lift his hat from his head and wipe the sweat-stained band.

Steam rose from the gray, speckled coat of the horse, and the animal stumbled occasionally. Soft echoes came to him, discordant sounds of restless animals. Ben dropped the reins and slipped from the gray, waited for a moment trying to sight in on the noise. It came from below him, over the edge of a dark-rimmed hole. On his belly he slid to the very edge. And below him were Nora's cattle, lowing their distress in being boxed in the small close-cropped canyon. The smell of burned hide and harsh smoke came to Ben. He wanted to get closer, but there well might be a guard. He waited for several hours, letting the dark cover him. Once he went back to the gray, who had found his breath and was pulling at mouthfuls of thin grass.

He tied the gray with the mecate, but left the horse bitted; another quick exit might be in order, and he could not count on the gray's cooperation. He worked his way back to the rim, closed his eyes, and settled his mind to listen for someone below.

He could hear nothing, no sounds of pursuit, no single rider keeping an eye on the restless cattle. Finally he took the challenge and rolled over the lip, working his way down the slanted wall, taking big handfuls of dry grass and small shrubs to balance his slide. The cattle immediately smelled him and moved cautiously away. The dark let him see little, but enough of the close mottled hides were near to see the fresh lines of a Wide Z brand, to distinguish the old white lines of the Stuart Slant S underneath. In a few days that fresh line would be gone and the cattle would belong to the Wide Z.

The climb back up the loose hillside was awkward and tiring in his high boots. He made a better detective on horseback, he thought wryly. The gray resented Ben and snapped at him as he wound the long mecate back and tied it to the horn. He slapped the threatening muzzle and mounted, eager to start the long ride back.

He needed Orton, or some lawman with authority, to come back here unseen and check the herd. They would have to butcher out one cow for proof. His mind kept going over and over the same thought, never giving him rest: this herd was Nora's survival and Tolliver's death. He rubbed the burn on his shoulder, still tender and swollen. The fire had taken too much of him; the trip down the mountain had taken the rest. But the gray had enough to bring them both back home.

Racking the gray in front of the slanted saloon, Ben scrubbed a hand across burning eyes. The place was boarded up, the single street deserted. In the short days since he had ridden through, the few folks left in this dying settlement had drifted on, leaving the town to finish its death alone, and leaving Ben without supplies to carry him over his backtrail.

A quick trip through the boarded-up buildings brought him two airtights of peaches, a rind of moldy bacon, and a weevil-infested bag of flour. It was something for his hunger, but not much. He packed the few items in his thin roll and mounted the gelding one more time.

This time he thought he heard an escaping sigh from the indestructable gray. As he rode past the shifting buildings, already crumbling without the support of human activity, Ben wondered why the departing people had bothered with the effort of boarding up their decaying property. Did they expect to return in a year, ten years, and find anything left of these few bits of lumber?

The trail started up toward the high and bitter pass. There would be snow up on top now, not much, perhaps, but enough to make the nights longer and the going icy. The image of Hattie Childress came to him. She would be warm through these late fall nights. He knew he was near the small cabin deep in the clearing, the yard around it hard-packed and swept clean, the gear hung carefully on nails, the paint mare fat and groomed to shine. The woman who lived there had blue eyes and a full mouth, a mouth that had held to his and drawn him in. Ben's thoughts stayed with the woman, leaving the gray to pick his way along the narrow and rock-strewn trail.

The horse turned a corner and brought Ben up against three riders, coming at him with rifles loosely held and barrel down. The four horses stopped dead and for that one moment no one spoke. The air came clear and cold, the silence drew too long. Ben thought of and discarded a hundred ideas: he faced three men he knew, Windy Dawes, Lug Bremen, and Mont Hackett—and he faced them with no handgun and his rifle wedged under his leg.

A suspended moment. Ben tightened his grip and drove spurs deep into gray, speckled flanks. The horse reared up and rammed hard into the close-bunched horses, sending Dawes's pretty mare to her knees, knocking Hackett's big bay against the thin roan of Bremen.

The gray charged into the thicket, fighting for cover. The horse ran with ears flat, head low. The side of the trail dropped suddenly and the horse and Ben went to their knees, then the gray lunged sideways into deeper growth. Ben's head slammed forward and then back with the changing momentum, smashed into a low-swinging branch. Darkness filled his eyes, then a burst of brilliant fire covered him.

The gray stumbled again, recovered, and stood still, head high, ears pricked. Down a steep drop was a small meadow ringed by dark fir, and the shadowed lip of a deep canyon at the edge of the grass. The gray jerked the reins from Ben's fingers, took two bucking strides through the trees. Ben forced stiffened fingers to close around the rifle beneath his leg. A hard jerk freed the weapon just as the gray suddenly gathered himself and pushed off from the slope, sailing out and down toward the bright grass below.

A shot aimed high at Ben's back caught the gray at the height of his leap, going in sideways through his body and coming out to the left between his front legs. There was no warning. Bright blood came from the rigid mouth, the horse dropped instantly to the rolling ground. Ben slammed to the hard, frozen earth, scrambling to get away from the broken mustang.

The slight body bounced and turned over, bounced again and disappeared over the dark side of the canyon. Shots ranged around Ben, seeking him as he watched the gray corpse go over the edge. And then he was alone with his rifle, with no protection from the gunmen above.

He got up and ran. He had no choice. Instinct turned him and he could see a rider bearing down on him, rifle held in one hand. Ben brought up his own weapon, took a brief moment to guess where the racing horse would carry its rider, and he squeezed off a desperate and lucky shot. The rider came off the runaway horse to land hard and lifeless on the hillside.

Before he got his second shot off, something cracked against the top of his head and he fell, loose and awkward. He was vaguely awake, aware of the pain flowering from his head, just able to hear the mumble of voices, feel footsteps hit the rutted ground, sometime after the echo of the rifle shot caught up to him.

Blood covered his eyes, burning them, bringing a red covering to what little he could see.

"Jesus God."

The voice wasn't familiar to him, but its meaning was clear. They had found their own man. Something nudged Ben, something with a sharp edge. Words ran over him, words with little meaning.

Mont Hackett stuck his boot toe less kindly into the sprawled body and shoved hard, lifting the fallen man over onto his back. Pale blue eyes showed beneath fluttering lashes, blood smeared across the gaunt face, but the fallen man made no effort to move.

Mont's anger rose. "This bastard took down Bremen. Good buddy for fifteen years now. Shot by this one."

The boot swung back, and another blow caught Ben under his arm, sliding him along the frozen ground. He grunted with the pain.

Windy Dawes was satisfied. They were supposed to find this man, bury him, and come home with the evidence. Already he had a fresh hide in his saddlebags, butchered off one of the Stuart beeves and now carrying a vented R Cross. But he didn't want to dig a grave up here, or cart a body. Perce had said not to. Just had to bring back the blotted brand as proof, and leave a dead man buried in the mountains.

Hackett's fury solved Dawes's problem. Hackett's book went again and again into Ben's inert body, each kick sending him closer to the edge of the narrow canyon. Ben could sense the blows, knew they must hurt, but could feel nothing. One last kick, and Ben Raynor's limp body rolled off the edge.

He knew he was falling, knew he would die when he hit bottom. He opened his mouth to scream his protest, but no sound came. He felt only the weightlessness. By a supreme effort of will he moved his arms, flailing about in the rushing air, seeking something to grab, to break his fall. But there was nothing.

Sounds went by his head, savaging his ears, screaming into his paralyzed brain. He could not respond, he could only wait. To reach bottom and his death.

He landed hard, flat on his back, arms outspread. He landed soft. Something gave beneath him, cushioning him. His head was wrapped in wetness, his outflung arms found steaming warmth. Something bristly rubbed against his fingers. He lay still for a long moment, then searched about in his darkness. His hands found an abrasive softness, then a slim ropy wetness, then a ridged core that rose and fell beneath his seeking fingers. A familiar shape, a rope, a high-pronged horn. His saddle.

He rolled his head, squeezed his eyes hard, then opened them against the pain. He was eye-level with gray hide, bristly short hair, woven lines of faded color, a high-cantled saddle. He was lying on the body of the ugly gray mustang, guts torn and spread to steam in the cold air.

Chapter Fifteen

Cable Orton watched as the rancher stepped down from the black and tied the restless horse snugly to the railing. He couldn't help but admire the lines of the big horse, and chuckled at the contrast of the animal's perfection stacked against his rider. Perce Tolliver was short, wide, stubby legged, carrying his close to sixty years with a defiant set to his back and a banked rage in his gray eyes. Cable Orton didn't much like the man.

It looked like he was here on business. Tolliver came into the small office and warmed himself at the comfort of a small wood stove. One snap of his wrist shook the light dusting of snow from a folded skin, and laid it out on the crowded desk, sending papers to the floor.

The town marshal willed himself not to respond: Tolliver's pale eyes were waiting to fight. Orton smiled at the belligerent rancher, then spoke his piece. The soft sounds belied the impact of his words.

"Whatever got up your tail, get it out quick and then get the hell out of my office."

He smiled again. The harsh words had lifted the offensive from the rancher, and it looked as if Perce didn't like it. But the man was willing to continue the game. There was only a moment's tightening of the deep lines at his mouth, then Tolliver gave his answer. He had yielded this round to the law.

"My foreman came in two days ago, brought this with him. We had got word that Raynor's no-good grandson was running cattle out beyond. Sent Windy and two men to check. Raynor got one of them, before they sent him over the edge. Found this in his roll. Tells it all." He paused to underline his next words.

"Just wanted you to know." A wicked light came to the clear gray of his eyes. "Wanted you to know we taken care of the cattle thief. Nice and clean."

Before Cable could turn the hide over, Tolliver punched his silver hat down on the faded red hair and was gone from the office. The marshal had gotten ahead of him for a bit, but that hide would put the man where he belonged. The hide and the set-to up in the hills.

Tolliver wiped his damaged hand over his face and grimaced, then laughed in the cold air. He wanted a drink. Early, maybe—but that hide and its message gave him the right to celebrate and be damned to them all.

The hair side showed a fresh R Cross brand, crude but clear, a legal mark. The flesh side, beginning to rot, offering a taint of decay in the warm room, showed the blotted S Slant underneath. Not an easy change, but a good man could do it well enough. Butchering would be the only way to read out the two brands; this work had been done by an expert.

Cable glowered at the evidence before him and the death tale from the arrogant rancher. Raynor dead, a Traveling T hand shot down. Two men left up in the mountains, with only this coarse hide in his hand to bear out the word of a self-styled avenger. Orton frowned, his heavy face drawing in on itself, fleshy lips folding up to broken nose, eyes disappearing behind drawn lines.

The evidence was in his hands. But the story behind it smelled. He grimaced at the unintentional pun and threw the heavy leather to a corner of the small office. Two men left up in the mountains. He resisted the memory of the copper-headed man buried under winter snow. He was going to miss that one.

Damn being confined by town. He would have to wait. Wait out the end of the story. Snow was coming to the basin. It would all have to end here in town. He slammed shut the door and stood on the walk, following with his eyes the steps Tolliver must have taken. Then he dug a booted heel in hard to gouge the wood beneath him, and went in the other direction. The tale would spread, and he wanted to count its passage.

Nora's head rocked violently as she refused to hear the story from its bearer. Nancy Ridgeway was adamant, firm in her facts, and shook her head back at the obstinate woman in front of her. Emily stood by, numbed by the condemning words sounding so innocent in the mouth of the soft, round, proper Mrs. Ridgeway. But the woman would not let go.

"Why, yes, it is true. I heard George talking with the doctor. They are both very upset, deceived by that man they took in. Why, that man took us all in, stealing your cattle, my dear, taking your livelihood from you and after you had given him a job, sat up

171

with him, took care of him. I don't know."

A shake of her careful curls, and Nancy Ridgeway stepped her way to the street, preparing to cross back to her side and go home. She had talked enough for today, she thought. Why, those two poor women, how they must suffer.

Somewhere along with her distress over the story circulating through the town—the tale of Ben Raynor's defeat by the dogged efforts of Mr. Tolliver's men and the subsequent exposure of his perfidy—the facts of this same man's heroic actions were lost to Mrs. Ridgeway. There was no one to defend him. The honors now went to Perce Tolliver.

The word spread. And Cable Orton, standing on the worn planks of the raised boardwalk, counted the time and noted the strength of the condemnation. The telling had come from Tolliver, and the heated retelling was confirmation of his growing power. Orton stayed at his post outside the office and watched the bunches of people come together, split apart, and regather in varying numbers.

"Marshal, you don't seem taken with the news. Why not? Everyone else is convinced."

The voice was so gentle, holding an inflection of doubt and warmth together. Cable did not turn to the speaker, but kept his eyes on his town.

"Wasn't in him. He's up there in those damn mountains. Dead. Shot by Dawes and that other one, Hackett. That there hide don't mean nothing. Ben Raynor may have been a drifter, running from his past. But he wasn't a thief."

Cable turned then to the woman standing behind him. Emily Chapman's face showed the tracks of tears, but her eyes were bright and dry. Feelings he thought hidden came to him. His big hand rested lightly on the faded colors of her sleeve, just barely touching, offering its support. The dark head came up; the wild violet eyes found Cable's own dark brown.

"Marshal, he touched Nora, not me. I've been waiting for you but didn't know it."

She carefully lifted the big hand from her arm; before she let it drop she pressured hard into the broad knuckles, then allowed the sheer weight of the hand to bring itself down. Nora would need her now. The man could wait, had waited all this time and would wait longer. She headed back to the wagon, watching the team already fighting the heavy hand on the leathers.

Nora's eyes burned into Emily. Her hands shook on the reins, drawing the mares' heads high, sending twitches to their tender mouths.

"Damn them all. And damn Tolliver most of all. I told him Ben had gone looking. But I was concerned for Ben and trusted Tolliver. Now Ben is gone and that sly old man takes in the praise for unmasking a thief. And we still don't have our herd."

Tears fought through the flush, running in thin lines down the angular face to gather at the soft collar of her coat. She took a backhand swipe at the wetness, then picked out her buggy whip and shook the mares to a trot. A shudder escaped her, then she caught hold of the feeling and clamped down. And drove the mares faster towards home.

He'd been here before. A long time ago. The face so

close to his did not belong to him, but he knew it. The face laughed at his efforts to reach it, moved away from flailing hands. Then Ben Raynor remembered.

His hands stopped in midair, reached out slowly and rested on the warm, dry skin of Hattie Childress's face. She slid one hand along her cheek, brought her mouth to the damp palm and bit down, drawing a small red circle of marks on the calloused underside of the scarred hand. Ben yelped, brought his hand back and tried to slap her. She smiled at him. The weakness still held him, but he was getting better.

"Guess you know where you is all right. Now do you recollect me? And where you been the past few days?"

Ben closed his eyes, searching inside for an order to his scattered memory. The wet gray hide washed with blood, shots fired, forever falling. Then bits of climbing, sharp rock tearing at his hands and knees. Somehow he had known where he was headed. That small cabin in the clearing, set in its neat yard, penning in an old paint mare.

How long ago. He had no idea, rolled his head side to side in fury at his lack. Pain came at him, dormant pain that had been waiting for such carelessness. Hattie watched the rolling head, watched the pain come to the thin, dark-bearded face. What he was fighting she could not help.

Ben ran a hand weakly across his face; he was hot to the touch, burning. Old and too-familiar images came at him, images he had put behind him. He squeezed his eyes hard, driving away the pain. Hattie's dark face stayed with him behind reddened eyelids, Hattie's face mixed up with Nora Stuart. He

174

gave up the fighting and drifted back to a restless sleep.

Ben struggled to sit up, then became conscious of his nakedness. Of being in a deep bed covered with a careful-patterned quilt. He opened sore eyes and looked at the beautiful face so near his. Hattie Childress.

Unexpectedly she leaned down to him and took his mouth with her small teeth, gently teasing his lips. She brought both hands to his face and eased him back down into the soft pillows, letting go of his mouth very slowly.

"Mister, you get from me just what I want to give. Now is no time for this. I listened to you for 'most two days now. That woman back where you from, she's the one you belong to. You and me, we ain't to be together for a lasting time, just for pleasuring. But that one you want forever."

A sad smile, very slight, came to the thin face. Hattie dug a hand deep into her blond hair.

"You give me a lot, mister. You give me what I want. Now I know what Ma was speaking. You rest up. Soon as you can, we taking the mare and be gone."

Questions came to Ben, of all the particulars, of what had happened, of his injuries and how long. Hattie pushed on his chest, elbowing him into the softness of the bed. She shook her head.

"Nothing but time now. You sleep some more, then we talk."

A day later Ben grabbed the spoon from Hattie's hand and threw it across the room. "Damn it, girl, food. Not this gruel for children." Hattie only grinned at his temper. There had been concern for him the past days, distress that he lay so passive, staring up under his bandaged head, seeing nothing yet awake and aware. This anger was a good sign.

Ben sat up fast and swung his legs over the side. Unconcerned about nakedness, he stood up, shaky, weak, but finally on his feet. He growled at the pleasure obvious on the small woman's face.

"You've been baiting me, trying to get me on my own." His face turned sheepish through the anger. "Let's get my clothes before I freeze, and then get moving. I got to get back to Isherton's and get something that puts Tolliver with the herd. Lost too much time now to get the law. Dawes and his crew will have their own story, got to have something . . ."

Ben heard his voice go thin, far away. He stepped forward blindly like a gored steer, went to his knees and hit the dirt floor hard on his face. He heard Hattie's light giggle, felt her wiry arms tug at him. But she got further and further away, and he knew nothing.

This time he took it slowly, put his feet out to the ground in easy steps, not blundering but cautious like an old fighting bull. He couldn't find Hattie. There was no sign of her in the small cabin. He could see a light-colored piece of board resting on the slab table. Short steps took him nearer; the back of a crude chair gave him support as he picked up the wood. Lettered across it in charcoal were a few hard-to-read words: *"gon to help bout cows back son sta put. Hatti."*

The closed door was within reach. It took a long

time to reach it. The rawhide latch pulled easily and the door opened. It had been a long time for him inside. Snow covered the packed yard, fresh snow showing no tracks. Last night's snow. No paint mare loafed in the pen, and there was no sign of Hattie anywhere.

He was cautious as he went back inside. Dimmed coals in the fireplace told Ben she had been gone overnight. The cabin carried only a hint of warmth, but he had been dressed in woolen shirt and pants, and the bed was heaped in old blankets. Hattie had prepared him well.

He searched through the few shelves in the cabin, and found Hattie's supplies. There was stale flatbread and dried meat, enough to keep him for two or three days, until Hattie came back. He tore at the jerked beef, chewed slowly with stiffened jaw, and felt an echoing pain through his head. Nothing in the cabin told him how long he had been here, and rubbing a hand over his face told even less. Not even a beard length to guess at. Hattie knew all a man's needs.

He must have gone to sleep again. Hattie burst into the cabin, spoke loudly at the man slumped at the rough table.

"You up. Good. Time now to work on you getting stronger."

She held up a dirty piece of paper. "You wanted something on that Tolliver fellow, something putting him with Isherton. Well, I got it. Rode quiet-like to his ranch middle of the night. Snuck into a big room, full of papers. Seen your name scratched on this here

177

bit. Looked like the word I kept seeing in those papers in your jumper. Ain't got much schooling but I know the letters. Figured it would mean something to you so I brought it along, with a hide right outta his barn. Got his Wide Z laced over that Stuart brand."

Ben reached for the paper and laid it on the table surface. He smoothed the bit carefully, taking time to iron out the crisscross of wrinkles. His name leaped up from the hastily written note—a note signed with Tolliver's hasty scrawl:

"Ish, cut out couple of that herd, blot the R Cross over Stuart's. Man name of Raynor's looking for the herd. Dawes will take care of him. Give Dawes what he wants. Perce."

Not much, just a dirty bit of paper carrying a few words. But they were enough to pin the rustled herd and his own murder on the arrogant rancher. Ben read the note again and turned to look at Hattie. Before he could speak she beat him to the words.

"This be what you want. I know it. Your face tells me. You going to leave now and take the mare. But give her a day's rest. She be old and 'nother trip be too much right now." Her face softened. "Stay with me. Tomorrow is soon enough. Stay with me tonight."

The bright blue eyes told him all; the thin face, winter pale, was hungry. He could not leave her.

He could only reach for her and stroke her face; she leaned into the motion, bringing her hand up to cover his. Slowly, stiffly, he stood in front of the woman and tugged at her arm, pulled her to him, and gently, ever so carefully, brought her into his arms. Her head fitted in the space under his chin; her arms went around him tight. They swayed against each other in

178

silence. Then he felt her sigh, twice, and push herself away.

Hattie Childress stood and looked at the man before her, a man who wanted another. She tugged at his gray-streaked copper hair, fingered the newly healed slash across the top of his head that soon would come in white. Her words were gentle.

"You never asked. I found you by the clearing edge. Hands all torn, pants hanging from your legs, all covered in blood. You didn't know me, tried to run. But I hauled you back here on the mare, spent two days quieting you."

She lightly fingered the red swollen line. Ben caught his lip in a jab of pain.

"This was bad. 'Most to kill you. But you're all right now. Right enough to go to that woman."

Ben came around under the tugging fingers to follow Hattie to the narrow bed with the soft pillows.

The paint mare snorted in the cold morning air as Ben jerked the stiffened leather cinch and planted a knee in the bulging sides. He winced as a stab of pain shafted through his head, sending white dots around his vision. Hattie saw his confusion.

"You ain't healed yet, Ben. There's snow up top; you need to heal, never mind riding through that. Stay longer, with me."

Ben winced again at the longing in Hattie's words. But today he was riding over that mountain and back to the distant basin where Perce Tolliver thought he was the new king. He mounted the mare and reined her around to face the white, shadowed peak up ahead.

His fingers went to his breast pocket, securing the bit of paper inside, wrapped with other bits in an oilskin pouch. Then he glanced down at Hattie Childress. She knew it had to be today, not tomorrow. She just didn't want to know.

The good-byes had been said over and over. So Ben put spur to the wooly sides of the tobiana mare and jogged from the small cleared yard, not looking back until he had found the faint trail up to the peak and could look down at the faraway brown cabin almost hidden in the trees. A dark dot still stood in the yard. He lifted an arm and waved once, then turned the mare and rode deeper into the dry cold hills.

Chapter Sixteen

Damn him. Damn the man's gall. Damn him forever. Nora Stuart's head came up from the paper in front of her. A hand scoured her tired eyes roughly, as if to wipe away the fury. Perce Tolliver. Damn him.

She chided herself for the unladylike swearing, then grinned ruefully. Every time she thought of Perce Tolliver, she swore. She'd started that day in town when she heard the story he had spread. Had kept on swearing later when he'd ridden out to their ranch to offer his concern over the loss of the herd, the betrayal of their hired hand, and then she'd flowered into some more violent and colorful language in her head when he sat down to discuss the party.

And here she was, finishing the lists he needed, while Emily had gone to town. Nora couldn't help but smile again to herself. Emily had taken to town quite often lately, and always ended by visiting that big marshal. She had once justified the visits by some nonsense about tracking the herd, but Nora had only had to look at the blush across her pretty face to know the truth: It was time for Emily, and Cable Orton had the strength.

Not knowing the truth about Ben Raynor dug at Nora every moment. That same Marshal Orton had come to her and spoken his mind with great reluctance: He believed that Ben had ridden out to find the herd, not to rustle it. And had died in the attempt. She told the marshal she believed that Ben would be back. She wanted to believe he would be back.

Orton had only looked sadder at her words. So she had kept her faith silent, and swore under her breath at the arrogant son of a bitch who had set all this in motion.

The party was next week, six days from today, out at the Jackman ranch. Cable Orton was coming to take them both to the dance. Tolliver wanted them there by his side, to greet the guests, but Nora had refused that honor. Banking her growing anger, she'd spoken something about her sister, the marshal, ranch chores, and chaperons. Of course, the man had offered to send a hand by to take care of whatever needed doing. But Nora had sighed and refused, not looking into the clear gray eyes, afraid he would see the hate. Six days, and the party would be over.

The paint mare labored through the deepening snow. Ben sat quietly in the old saddle and urged the mare on with soft words and curses. He had walked alongside her until his legs had given out, until the white dots had taken his vision. The mare wheezed in the thin air, and drops of her breath froze on her whiskers, giving her a Christmas beard.

Then the mare stopped abruptly, throwing Ben against the high pommel, digging the horn into his belly. He reached down and stroked the ice-covered neck, then wiped a blanket-wrapped hand across his face to dislodge the buildup of frost. The mare snorted and trembled, but would go no further, humping her back against the dig of spurs. Ben cursed under his breath.

The small figure of the old paint mare and the rider were barely visible in the swirling white dust. In two days the mare had brought Ben to the height of the pass, to the rock-tumbled meadow beneath the high peaks. He could see the dark line of stunted trees at the rim of the meadow, trees that would shelter them both for the night, trees that marked the downhill side of their passage.

It took time to get down from the mare, then he lifted her head by the bit shank. Ice spiked her eyelashes, hung from her long whiskers, rattled against the metal bit shank. Pushing and prodding he hauled the mare across the small meadow, stumbling over hidden rocks, Ben doing the cursing for them both. The mare plodded behind the bent figure of the man, numbly following where he led. Down into the thin treeline Ben pushed them, searching for a rock to shelter, for dropped branches to use as fuel.

Standing near the bulk of a broken rock, Ben slipped the bit from the old mare, loosened the cinch, then fought the stiff leather strings that tied his roll to the cantle. The huge rock offered some break from the wind, and Ben used his last bit of strength to pick up blown scraps of wood for a fire. The mare shoved her head into his side and stayed with him, seeking warmth from his fire and his body.

Slowly, hand trembling, he measured out a handful

of oats for the paint, and tore at the long strips of dried meat that Hattie had sent with him. The mare echoed his chewing motions, making soft, content noises.

In the morning he laboriously melted snow over the small fire to water the mare. She drank the warmed liquid carefully from the small pot, then lipped his hand to search out a few bits of stray grain. He shoved the heavy head aside and took his own drink, then poured the remaining water over the flames, sending steam quickly into the frigid air.

Even with the light snow blowing around him, Ben knew the trail, knew where he was. A thin line dropped through the trees, winding around the heavy rock and going forever downward. On this side of the mountain range the trees grew denser, the land sloped more precariously toward the basin somewhere out beyond.

Ben tugged on the bridle line and urged the patient mare with each step. He would need her once they reached the more level valleys surrounding the springs and the quick trail down to the Stuart ranch and town. Till then he would go slowly, and nurse the old mare along.

His mind wandered. The days behind him that had brought him here, the fire, a letter sent searching, the two sisters. The old man. It had all begun with the old man. Ben tried to smile, cracking the ice forming on his mouth, frosting his beard. The old man with his determination to hand on the ranch, to continue life beyond his own death.

His thoughts touched on Hattie, and shied away from what she had been. Her caring, the touch of her, the feel of her skin. He stopped thinking back, and watched the path ahead.

The trail widened imperceptibly, opening up through high-reaching trees to a narrow line along a canyon rim. He had made it. This was where that one telltale hoofprint had been. He unwrapped the wool around his hands and did up the paint's cinch. The old mare nudged his shoulder, impatient and resentful.

After a time he swung up into the saddle and steadied himself on the fork. Those damned white dots covered his eyes, sent his head spinning. He waited patiently while the specks cleared. He'd learned this patience with Hattie, learned to wait out the spinning storm in his head, learned to breath easy and just wait.

Then he set the mare trotting through thinning snow down the hard rock trail. Urgency drove him. He had taken his time crossing the pass, had husbanded the mare's strength for this moment, so he drove the horse recklessly across the smaller valley, the wind-cleared grasses thick and life-giving. The cattle were gone, the remainder herded down nearer the ranch.

But the proud bay stallion and his mares stared in bewilderment at the horse and rider invading their home. The bay came out from his shelter, bugling a call in defiance of the interlopers. The paint mare responded to the cry, swerving toward the band with a suddenness that caught Ben off guard.

His weight slipped to the left, unbalancing the heavy-footed mare, who lurched and went to her knees. Ben dug his right leg into the hard leather saddle and threw himself to the mare's off shoulder, fighting for balance. Horse and rider floundered in the slippery, hoof-packed ground; the mare took scrambling strides on her knees, then suddenly stopped. Ben slid to the right, straightened himself, and rode out the lurch as the mare regained her feet. He grinned in self-mockery: to come all this way back and almost lose everything to a flatfooted mare's love. . . .

The bay stallion took two more strides toward them and snorted a high fluttering sound meant to entice the old mare to his harem. Ben laid the reins hard against the frosted neck, pulling the mare away from her kin. Two strides and he knew the trouble. He slipped off and ran a hard hand down the near foreleg of the mare. Through the thick winter hair protecting her leg he could feel heat, a swelling that grew under his fingers. The stumbling, wrenching fall had pulled something, and the old mare was useless.

Stripped of gear, the old mare looked at her companion, blew softly through iced nostrils, and limped towards the band, finally lifting the foreleg and hobbling the last steps on three legs. Ben eyed the horses. Most were old mares well in foal, with this year's foals by their sides, not much better to ride than the lamed paint. The rest were a scattering of yearlings and two-year-olds, unbroken and barely able to carry a rider's weight.

The bay stallion recognized Ben. He knew man, had been well started and used some before being turned out for his duties. Years spent in this valley and the small green graze on the basin had kept him familiar with man. He did not retreat as Ben walked toward him, coils of rope in his left hand, a small loop held easy in his right.

The bay only pinned his ears forward, their tips almost touching, as he listened to the soft noise coming from the blanketed figure nearing him. There was nothing threatening in the actions, but the stallion grew restless, lifting one muscled foreleg to paw the ground, signaling it was time for the man to back away.

Ben came too close to the big horse. The bay reared, sending a warning at the creature who now threatened his band. Ben stayed motionless, then whistled sharply through his teeth. The bay came down hard; Ben whistled again, adding a higher pitch to the sound. The bay stallion was still, ears sharp, eyes fixed on the confusing figure in front of him.

This was his chance. Ben threw an underhand loop that settled on the crested neck just behind the fine ears, and pulled the line tight. Then a quick twist of his wrist sent an underhand loop that doubled and caught the stallion around his muzzle, creating in effect a halter for the horse.

The bay went wild. On towering hind legs he pulled back at the harsh pressure covering his tender nose. The immediate pain brought him down, then he reared again, in panic this time, fighting the tightening band that bruised his soft skin. But the pain only got stronger, more immediate, as he strained against the pressure. The bay charged without coming back to the ground, springing coiled quarters to launch himself at the tormentor before him.

Ben spun from the slam of the horse against his side, slipped in the uncertain footing and rolled fast, holding desperately to the line. The bay slid in the snow, rolled back over his quarters, and struck out at the man-figure dark against the torn white ground. A flint-hard hoof caught Ben in the hip, numbing his leg, sending him rolling over in the icy grass.

The bay stallion squealed in his fury, mouth open wide with anger as he fought to sink teeth into the weak flesh of his captor. His jaws found a bundled arm; the teeth tore through a wad of wool to find the muscle beneath. Tears came to Ben's eyes at the immediate pain. He struck back at the bay muzzle so close to his face, beating the fine skin with a coil of hard rope.

The horse jerked away from the savage pain, tearing away with him the sleeve of the coat and the jumper underneath, leaving a ridge of bloody marks in Ben's upper arm. So close to the horse he could see the fine veins of rage standing on the wooly-coated neck, Ben took his chance. He grabbed for the rope swinging from the chiseled head, yanked down on the welted muzzle, and wound his free hand into the coarse black mane.

Trapped in the heavy coat, stiff and slowed by the pummelling the bay had given him, Ben swung up on the crouched back of the stallion and hooked a leg over the broad red rump.

The mane secured him. He wove the strands around his stiff fingers and dug his boot toe under the elbows of the animal. The stallion's stunned surprise did not last long. The crouching animal roared with the indignity and came up to a precarious rear, pawing at the air, balanced on the slippery ground with spread hind feet, forelegs tearing wildly at the air. Ben crouched over the bay's withers, drew his legs up along the shoulders, and planted his spurs in the stallion's ribs.

The bay came down with stiff forelegs, fighting for his head with demonic fury. Ben hauled on the crude war bridle as the bay snaked his head, desperate for his freedom. His spurs raked punishing strokes across the sweaty sides. Unable to get his head, the bay ran for his freedom. Tearing through the small valley, the horse bugled again and again in frenzied screams. Ben no longer had any semblance of control. The big stallion raced wildly, kicking out in futile attempts to free himself. But the unwanted burden stayed imbedded on his back, yanking at the rope bridle, tearing delicate flesh, spurs gouging ever-widening circles of blood from heaving sides.

Ben's eyes closed against the cold wind; he drew in on himself, burrowing deeper into the thick mane and flowing shoulders. If he ever let go, the stallion would tear him to shreds with teeth and hoof. So he clung to the crazed horse, conscious only that he could not let go.

Habit took over as exhaustion slowed the stallion's rage. The bay found the worn path to the ranch, and memory of kind hands and sweet hay fought through the red haze of his brain. He struck out on the trail, whickering at his mares who were standing together in bewilderment. It took the old red mare, burns still oozing serum on her back, to pick up a slow ponderous trot, with a bay filly following her. The herd started slowly, then habit took over, and they knew they were going home.

Ben lifted his face from the heavy mane. Beneath

him the great body of the stallion slowed, turned, settled into a tired walk. Ben felt every muscle across his back; his right forearm burned painfully. He turned his head very slowly. Blood had congealed along his arm, a thin thread still trickling from the circle of torn flesh.

Beneath him the stallion trembled as he loosened one hand to stroke the salt-crusted neck. Slowly, very cautiously, he lowered his legs, wincing as the bruised muscle along his hip stretched long. He could see the back of the Stuart ranch, could see the peak of the new barn. The bay knew he was home, and broke into a ragged trot that brought the herd into the small yard.

The bay turned at knee pressure and went into the large holding pen. Ben slipped from the wet back and removed the head rope in one awkward move. The freed bay did not take the advantage to resist his imprisonment, but gratefully walked deep into the high-walled corral and to an empty hayrick. The mares followed.

Every step was an effort for Ben. It took time, too much time, but he made several staggered trips from the barn to drop hay into the ricks. The silence carried him, enveloped him in a soft hand, eased the numbness deep in him. The fight and violent ride had sapped him to exhaustion.

Planning the next moves came hard. He needed things: a jacket, horse, saddle, a gun. Then town, the big face of Cable Orton. He found the brown gelding inside the barn, stalled near the blue dun and a chunky appaloosa. The team of roan mares was gone, which meant the ranch was deserted. It explained why no one had come to the commotion. Ben stopped in his feeble attempt to saddle the brown. There was more he had to do.

He slapped the big saddle on the horse, staggering slightly under the weight, fitted a hackamore to the wise head, and led the horse outside. It was easier to walk with the animal to the house than to contemplate trying to mount and ride the few steps. Once would be enough.

Clothes—he needed clothes. The drafty house made him aware of the many tears and holes in his jacket and pants. Aware that strips of faded cloth hung from his arm, that he could feel the cold air on his leg, and that blood had stiffened the coat, blood now beginning to thaw and drip. There was a place in this house where he could find clothing. Man's clothing. . . .

In Nora's room, where she still kept her husband's shirts, pants, even an old pair of boots. Clean clothes were packed away, waiting to be cut down for working clothes. He stood in the sparsely furnished room, swaying against the throbbing in his head and arm, the stiffness of his leg. There was a scent to this room, a feeling of Nora beyond the big sturdy marriage bed and vivid blue dress hanging from a peg. There was a vague and fleeting shame that he had come to her privacy without her knowledge. He turned blindly in a quickened distress to leave the room, and banged up against the doorframe.

The pain brought him back, pain in the burning arm that left him gasping, but alert. It was whiskey he needed now, to clean the wound and kill infection. Then clean clothes, and the brown gelding waiting outside. There was no time for thoughts or memories; he had to get to the law and deliver that small bit of wrinkled paper.

The cork gave him trouble, but it gave way and he tilted the bottle to swallow three times, coughing when the fire hit his belly. The torn shirt made a good rag, and he craned his head around to inspect the arm. There was little he could do for the swollen red flesh except pour whiskey into the hole and bind it with the remnants of shirt.

He tipped the bottle over his arm; the whiskey dribbled out, then rushed and flooded through the circle of blood. Ben sat down fast on the cracked leather sofa where he had spent so much time. His head swam; white spots circled through his eyes. He blinked back the water, then grunted and poured the rest of the liquor over the wound.

Sweat covered his face, rivulets ran down inside his longjohns. Ben sat in the darkened house alone, head between his knees, fighting the weakness that took him. This day wasn't ready to end yet. Finally he could stand, and he walked through the shadows back to the bundled clothes to dress. The brown was waiting, a good friend. Ben stayed in the house a moment longer. Something was missing.

A weapon. He wasn't going to go up against Tolliver and his crew without a weapon. He found an old Winchester, scabbard and shell belt hanging beside it, in a small room that had to be an office. There were books spread out on the desk, papers piled in staggered groups. And that faint smell that defined Nora Stuart. This was her room now, her ranch, her office where she struggled to run her life. The loss of that herd would cripple her. He had to finish.

On the second try he mounted the patient brown and turned toward town. He patted the unfamiliar weapon beneath his left leg and found his thoughts going back to the small woman beyond the pass. She would laugh at him for his weakness, and then join him to fight.

Town came quickly. Ben angled the brown to the unlit office of the marshal. Dismounting, one hand went automatically to the small oilskin pouch still wadded in his jumper pocket. He'd salvaged the jacket minus one sleeve. It was all that was left of his own belongings.

"Marshal ain't here, mister. Where you been? Whole darn town's out to the Jackman place, whirling around and drinking up Tolliver's fine booze. Marshal locked me up, told me to tell any idiot that came here to ride out to the ranch. You got a smoke, a bottle? How 'bout finding them keys and letting me loose. Ain't done nothing."

The whining voice had come through the dark from inside the warmed room. Ben struck a match and picked up a lantern hanging near the door. A small man, wrapped in a blanket, sat in the only cell in the back of the office. His voice matched the thin face and filth-crusted clothes. Ben smiled, a short smile that took the grimness from him. The man quieted down as he watched Ben walk to his cell. They eyed each other through the shadowed bars, and Ben spoke softly: "You tell me again, where is the marshal?"

The small man sat back further into his blanket, the whine in his voice growing stronger. "I told you, out to the Jackman place. Whole town is there for a

193

shindig. But not me. I got to sit here and mind the store. That's what the marshal calls it. Me, I think I'm in jail."

The voice slowly shut down its whine. Ben's pale eyes watched the scrawny face as its owner sought some pity for the tale from the man on the other side of the key. The reddened brown eyes widened very slowly as the man finally recognized the face of the man who was before him. Panic almost shut down his voice.

"But you be dead. That's what Tolliver's man said. You stole that herd from Miss Nora and they shot you. Gosh darn it, you be back from the dead."

The voice trailed off, and the man put his hands in front of his face, flapping them as if to shoo away the ghost. The "ghost" grinned at the foolishness.

"Thanks for the information. You take care now. And keep safe."

In the office he found papers and tobacco in a desk drawer. Tossing them to the shaking man safe in his cell took little time. "Have your own party on the marshal. Sorry there ain't a bottle."

Outside, standing again by the patient brown, Ben contemplated what was ahead. It all would fit. The whole town out at the Traveling T for a whirl, at Tolliver's invite. And he had a bit of paper that would end the dance.

His pale eyes widened in the dark; a faint grin tugged at his mouth. It wasn't too often that a ghost got to dance at a party.

Chapter Seventeen

The angular man stood high above his audience on the raised flooring, and grinned down at the gathering of folks waiting for him to finish tuning his fiddle and get to serious music-making. Sweat dripped from his chin, pooling in his beard and at the back of his collar. He dragged a patterned bandanna across his face and waved it over his head. The banjo player behind him ran eager fingers across his instrument; the two men found their chords and began again.

The night had already been long, and there was more still to come. No one wanted to return to their dark houses and begin the morning. Nora's foot tapped to the music in spite of her continuing anger. It was impossible to put the music aside and keep her mind on Perce Tolliver. A red-faced cowhand came near, stopped, and moved his high-heeled boots in their own nervous dance.

"Miz Stuart, you do me the honor of this here dance?"

His voice broke on the question, and he backed

away slowly as if already afraid of the answer. Nora politely nodded her head yes and put out her hand. No need to punish the boy for something he did not control. They spun out to the barn floor and joined the others in a bright whirl.

This time Emily Chapman was not the center of the dance. Word had gone around the small community that Cable Orton and Nora Stuart's beautiful sister were walking out. When and how no one knew. But the word had gone out.

The men left her alone and Emily enjoyed the change. She could watch the dancers without being begged for each dance. Cable stayed near her, spending the time with her but not joining the dance. He did not speak, just watched the floor with tired brown eyes as if something displeased him. Emily could see her sister's bright dress flutter in and out of the bending and swaying crowd, saw her grim face unravel with the motion, watched her steps lighten as the dance brought her pleasure.

There was a question in Emily's gaze. Ben Raynor was frozen up somewhere beyond the mountains; she was here and dancing, having put aside her fears. Cable stood behind Emily, face high over her shoulder, watching for something she did not see. She was tied to the man without words.

Tension built in her; then a rough hand enveloped hers, tugged gently, and led her to the floor. Out of step in the gay rhythm, Cable wrapped her with strong arms and lowered his head to hers. They waltzed slowly around the edge of the huge barn, sliding between the watchers on the side and the eager dancers.

Ben tied the brown gelding at the edge of the waiting horses, some still harnessed, others loose-tied with only a halter and line. He checked the cinch and eased the borrowed Winchester in its boot. The music drew him, the laughter and melted words something he had missed these two years.

He could watch from an unglassed window, and he marveled as the dancing grew wilder and voices pitched higher. The town of Gladstone and its neighbors were inside. Ben waited in the cold. He was waiting for one woman who would dance with him. He stayed in the shadows outside the vibrating barn and fought a silent, bitter battle with the wounds that threatened to take away the next hour from him.

Cable bowed to Emily and moved away to stand next to Perce Tolliver, leaving her stranded in the activity. She watched as he towered over the seated rancher, saw his eyes glint with anger as he leaned down and spoke to the cowman, banal pleasantries to their host. The man was a constant surprise. They had danced in silence; then, just before leaving her to join Tolliver, he had proposed they marry. And she had answered yes without hesitation.

Now she wanted to breathe. She needed to be in the cold, hard air, to clear the confusion in her. Emily Chapman stepped outside and walked away from the light, a shawl wrapped around her for protection. A shape came near her, moving from the deep shadows of the barn. Indistinct and blurred, it was a man, and wearing a familiar coat. Walt Stuart's coat. But Walt was dead.

And so was this man. Light touched the pale face and she jerked back in shock. Ben Raynor looked into her widened violet eyes, eyes that so many months ago had read him and pleaded with Nora to let him stay, let him work. Now he had to convince her again. He spoke against her panic.

"Emily, listen. Please. Whatever Perce is saying, he's lying. He took the cattle. I've got proof here in my pocket."

He went to dig out the pouch, but Emily's small cold hand stopped him. Shock still held her, but she struggled to find the words.

"Ben, you're mad to come here. Tolliver will kill you. He's been talking that you took those cattle, changed the brands, sold them. He's even got a hide as proof. Said his men had left you dead up in the mountains. Dear God, Nora was right. You aren't dead."

Ben came closer to the woman. A yellow slash of light caught the deepened lines of his face, enhanced the dark rough beard, the new line of white through the copper hair. Emily reached up to run fingers softly in the curls, touching gently at the new white. He flinched, jerking his head back, and she could only guess at the pain.

"He did shoot you. They weren't lying. But you survived. Nora knew you had. She spoke of it to Cable and he doubted her. He never doubted you, Ben. He knew you would not take from us. You had no need. Cable is inside, waiting for something to happen. The whole basin is inside. Waiting and dancing."

"Let's help things along, Em. Will you have this dance with me?"

Ben Raynor shook off the bulky coat and stood in front of the lovely lady, bowed slightly as he had been taught, and offered her his arm. Emily caught her lower lip in her teeth, then jerked her head once sharply as if in agreement, and rested her hand on the canvas-covered arm. She noted, almost absently, that the other sleeve was gone from the faded jumper, then she smiled her best party smily at the thin, pale-eyed man beside her. Her dancing partner for the final waltz of the evening was the man who had burned for them, who had fought and died for them, and who would now face the last devil.

Her escort took one step and faltered, then took a long breath. Emily glanced sideways at him, fearful of what she would see. But the exhaustion in his face had been replaced by a flash of energy that would carry him through the minutes ahead. Emily pressed down on Ben's arm and he responded, picking up the walk, and pushed open the small side door.

The fiddle hit a waltz; the banjo joined in, its tinny sounds adding to the gaiety. Cable Orton looked for Emily. This music he could handle. His eyes roamed those waiting against the walls, then narrowed in disbelief. He could see Emily, her fine body swaying in brief and innocent contact with a small, fire-headed man wearing a one-sleeved jumper. The pair circled the large floor slowly, moving closer to the blocky rancher still seated near Cable. They never missed the steps of the dance.

Ben Raynor. Alive. Dancing in hesitant circles to the center of the party. Couples slowed, bumped in their confusion, then stopped. The music faltered with a broken beat, took up again in time with the few dancers left, then ceased altogether.

Ben Raynor. The name was whispered through the crowded barn, echoed along the sides. Came to rest at Perce Tolliver's empty chair. . . .

A slow smile drew across Ben's gaunt features as he faced the cowman. His voice was soft, the words drawn out and slow, thick with politeness, inviting the older man to come forward.

"Well, Mister Tolliver, understand you've been insulting my name, putting it out that I'm a thief."

Ben glanced at the marshal, next to the short rancher but oddly detached from the scene, his face stilled. Ben sought the man's eyes, held to the contact, asking his question.

Orton nodded only once, returned the quick smile. He had declared himself out; now Ben could concentrate on Tolliver.

Perce's voice cracked with anger:

"Raynor, you got gall coming here. Marshal's got proof that you're the rustler. You killed one of my men. You might as well be in jail."

Perce was fighting for time with his words, seeking an escape, using the time to match up the cool air of

200

the ragged man standing close-by, challenging him. He sought desperately for something.

"Marshal, you arrest this man. That's why you're here."

Orton slowly shook his big head. "Perce, you come in to my office, fill out a warrant, bring it to me from the judge, and then I'll think about that arrest. Right now you got nothing but a smelly hide and a live dead man. Nothing in that."

Blake Morse had been waiting for this moment, ever since he had ridden up the mountain with Dawes and the two drunks a long time back to move those cattle. He'd balked at going back to the Wide Z with a word from Tolliver, but had ridden his job and kept his mouth shut. Now something had come to him. Kill Raynor, and Tolliver belonged to him.

He watched from the darkened doorway as the lone man reached to his breast pocket, slowly brought out a package. Morse drew his pistol, raised, and sighted on the thin back exposed to him. He waited a moment longer to hear the words, savoring his final power.

Ben held out a hand, fingers holding a grimy and wrinkled scrap of paper. "Marshal, this is my side."

Perce panicked and reached for the paper. He recognized the smudged words. He extended his hand, stepping down from the platform to come closer to the younger man challenging him. Cable noted in a detached part of his mind how close two people could be to the same mold and yet be so different. He watched Ben Raynor smile as the older man took another step. Imperceptibly Raynor stepped back,

201

drawing Tolliver to the dance floor, away from his self-imposed throne. The outstretched hand never waivered.

"Boy, you give me that note. Now."

The stilled dancers crowding the floor shifted and settled on either side of the two men, closed around them, isolating them. Blake Morse cursed as he was crowded deeper into his corner, unable to shoot. He weighed his chances, listening to the murmurs around him, then slipped out a small side door. It was time to cut his losses and run. Perce Tolliver was finished.

Perce took a hard look at the man holding the rest of his life. The indifference was gone; the pale eyes had a purpose and a life that threatened his. Tolliver wasn't going to lose again, and never to a two-bit son like this one. But he could not still an admiration for the man: beaten, burned, shot, and left to freeze. And still here, pushing for the end.

Perce gauged his chances and took them, stepped off his right foot, shifted his right hand to the bit of paper. Ben read the movement too slowly and twisted away from the reaching fingers—walked into the round barrel of a small, unseen pistol that rammed into his ribs.

Perce's voice was gentle: "Boy, you give me that note, right now." The hammer clicked as it was pulled back. The sound was muffled by flesh. The circle of onlookers pushed closer, not seeing the glint of metal up against Ben's side. And still Cable Orton did nothing. He could do nothing now except watch from the raised platform and wait. If that small hidden gun went off, a good many of the fine citizens of Gladstone would panic and run, a good many of the citizens would be hurt. Including Ben. Cable could only wait.

It had worked once before, had gotten him away from the riders up in the hills. Ben lurched forward into the round pressure, jamming up against Perce's hand. Then he wrenched sideways, bringing his right hand hard against the seamed face.

Perce jerked the trigger, then stumbled as the force of that hand kicked him backward. Fire ranged along Ben's side, tearing across his belly with a burning brand, smothered by the torn and patched jumper and billowing shirt.

Arnold Hiller gasped, turned in amazement to his neighbor, and put a hand to his side. It came away covered in blood. He brought the hand to his eyes, then touched it to his side again. A small scream came from dry lips, then Hiller slumped and fell against his neighbor, George Ridgeway.

The scream spread through the crowd. Tolliver forced his path wider as he pushed through the loosening townfolk. Stunned by the blow, Ben stood rooted for a long heartbeat. The fire ran its course, dimming to an ache. His left hand sought the damage. Little blood, just a long trail of singed flesh across ridged muscle.

He knew he had to move, to continue the battle. But his mind was muddled, slow-acting, thick and ponderous. He licked his mouth to bring moisture. The simple act focused his attention, and he knew again what he was doing.

He moved fast to follow Tolliver's path through the crowded barn. But not too close—he didn't want the second shot in the hideout gun to find another victim. Outside, the darkness bound his vision. Ben stopped to wait impatiently, listening for the sounds of Tolliver's escape. The line of horses shifted quietly. Beyond them, from a corral, came the irate snort of a stallion. It would be Tolliver's black. If the man got to that horse, then nothing would catch him tonight. Ben leaned into the chilled air and scurried head-down to the high fenced corral.

Nora made her way to the platform through the confused crowd of dancers. Her body still vibrated from the shock of Ben, of his being alive and with Emily. Cable Orton was still on the platform; Emily had joined him, a brown hand on his arm. Nora came directly to his line of vision, stood close in front of the hulking man.

"You. Do something. You can't let this go on." Her voice found its stride. "You saw him. Tolliver will kill him. You know it. It's your town, your job. His life. Please."

The marshal's voice was small and thin, unlike the strength in the man. "Nora, Emily, did you see it?" His question made no sense. Emily spoke: "Cable." Just that.

Cable Orton sighed deeply. He had been the only one to see. Ben Raynor had a driving need to finish with the older man. It was the end or the beginning of his life.

The marshal looked at the two women who were

tangled with his own life. He shook off the soft hand touching his, and stepped down to the floor. Hiller needed to be checked, and then he would go outside after Tolliver. If Ben lost, Tolliver could not be allowed to escape.

The black ran from Perce, circling the pen with long strides, fleeing the memory of heavy hands on his mouth, sharp spurs digging his sides. Perce cursed the horse, threatened him, fashioned a loop in the stiff rope and made his cast. The black stopped and whirled, the rope sliding from his back. Tolliver hastily curled the line, recast the loop, and caught the crested neck in an overhand toss. The black felt the circling pressure, and years of training froze him.

The pen rails were stacked close and high to make a durable pen. To get inside, Ben had to either go through the gate and make noise or be for a moment outlined and vulnerable at the top of the rails. He waited by the gate, looking for his moment.

Perce saw the shadow move, yanked on the rope to hold the stallion while he freed the small gun, and shot blindly. The bullet ricocheted, sending splinters into Ben's face. He ducked at the fragmented sound as another shot thudded into the post at chest height. And another. Perce Tolliver had an accurate eye.

The stallion snorted and backed away from the loud noise, bringing Perce's attention back to him. Ben shrugged out of his jumper, wound it into a hard wad, and threw it underhand to unfold and wrap around the raised black head of the already panicked horse. The stallion screamed and reared. Perce was forced to

205

fight the horse and take his eye away from the gate.

Ben ran through the gate into the corral, and dove at the struggling black shadows. His shoulder hit something soft, and hot breath crossed his face. Perce Tolliver grunted with the impact and went down, covered by the younger man.

The black found his freedom and reared again, striking out at the air. He came down on the tangled mass under his feet, reared again and fled from the struggle.

A gasp of pain escaped Ben as a sharp hoof landed on his back. The weight lifted but left its deadening mark. Tolliver, protected by Ben from the sharp hooves, flinched from the sound and at the same time fought to bring his right hand around, fingers clenched around the gun. The two-shot derringer had one bullet left. Ben's limp body smothered Perce, slowing his effort.

Ben could feel the body beneath him buck in an effort to get free. His mind willed his own body to act, but he seemed frozen. Tolliver finally slammed the short barrel against Ben's right arm, bringing fire back to the inflamed bite from the bay. The pain brought him alive. He shifted and found the right hand, wrapped both of his hands on the rigid forearm, and twisted.

The two bodies intertwined, tangled, rolled and bucked on the hard frozen earth. Tolliver's left hand rang again and again over Ben's ear, sending bright lights through his head, drawing him tight and close to the warm darkness. Blood ran down his right arm,

206

greasing his hand and loosening his hold on the short gun.

Then, for a short heart-stopping moment, Ben reached the edge. He felt nothing: his muscles did not respond to his will. Tolliver felt the change and shook the derringer free from the nerveless hands. He rolled from under Ben, rose to one knee, and hurriedly fired at the still form. Ben's body jerked from the impact, then relaxed.

Tolliver's triumphant grin was barely visible in the early dawn light. It was all his, now. He looked for the stallion, turning away from his foe for that one moment. Back on fire, stunned from the bullet's passage, Ben found his strength and came up fast on one knee to go for Tolliver. He slammed into the man's side and drove him back to the ground.

The gun broke from Perce's hand and flew into the dirt. Knees deep into Tolliver's chest, Ben pounded at the old face, striking again and again at the soft flesh, mashing the nose and drawing teeth and blood from the broken mouth. He did not feel his own knuckles split and crack in his fury. The body beneath his sagged, arched once, and was still.

"That's all, Ben. That's enough. You can't kill him."

Cable Orton had found the two men and stood ready to pull Ben from the defeated Tolliver. Blood bubbled and spilled from the ruined nose, the torn ear, and the swollen eyes closed in pain. But the man still breathed with short regular gasps. He would live.

Ben tried to stand, felt a sharp stab in his lower

back and side, and fell to his knees, too weary to make another effort. A strong hand reached to him, dug under his arm and gave him strength. He fought to his feet and stood alone. Bloodied, shot, beaten, but the final victor.

Voices grew around him. He waited for the one he wanted: a warm voice, concern carrying its sound across the grey shadowed pen—Nora Stuart.

He found her face in the light, shifted his shoulders and tried to walk. His feet gave way and he stumbled. She came to him, held his arm and put his weight against her own.

"Nora. I'm back. For good."

He leaned down and kissed the drawn mouth. It was time to start again.